Piece of Cake
published in 2013 by
Hardie Grant Egmont
Ground Floor, Building 1, 658 Church Street
Richmond, Victoria 3121, Australia
www.hardiegrantegmont.com.au

A CiP record for this title is available from the National Library of Australia.

Text copyright © 2013 Kate Forster
Illustration and design copyright © 2013 Hardie Grant Egmont

Design by Stephanie Spartels
Typesetting and text design by Ektavo

Printed in Australia by Griffin Press, an Accredited ISO AS/NZS
14001:2004 Environmental Management System printer.

The paper this book is printed on is certified against the
Forest Stewardship Council ® Standards. Griffin Press holds
FSC chain of custody certification SGS-COC-005088. FSC
promotes environmentally responsible, socially beneficial
and economically viable management of the world's forests.

1 3 5 7 9 10 8 6 4 2

Piece of Cake

kate forster

hardie grant EGMONT

1

There isn't a problem in the world that can't be soothed by chocolate, thought Lola as she licked rich ganache off the spoon in her hand.

'Put the spoon down and no-one will get hurt.' The voice came from the doorway of the kitchen. Lola turned to see her dad standing there.

'Back off, Dad,' she growled playfully. 'My cake, my party, my chocolate.'

'My cafe, my kitchen, my spoon,' he answered, flicking a tea towel at her bare legs.

Lola ignored him and turned back to her work, spinning the ganache-covered cake around on the decorating stand as she sprinkled fine edible gold dust over the top.

'So pretty,' she sighed, smiling at her handiwork. She wiped her cheek with the back of her hand, smearing a little chocolate on her face.

'It looks gorgeous, Lollipop, but are you going to help me make the actual dinner?'

'As if,' Lola scoffed, making a face and adjusting the tiny iced violets that were sitting on top of some nearby vanilla cupcakes. 'You know I only make food fit for queens.'

'Well, aren't you Little Miss Marie Antoinette,' said her dad good-naturedly.

Lola only liked to bake. The idea of rubbing a chicken with salt or tenderising a piece of meat wasn't an attractive one, and after all her visits to the fish market when she was small she knew that there was nothing elegant about shucking oysters or boning salmon.

David Batko, having trained in some of the best kitchens in the world, had once been the chef to watch – that is, until Lola came along. But if he missed the heady days in the kitchens of London and Paris, he never let on to his daughter. Rather than yearning for his past glory, he had thrown himself into running his inner-city cafe in Berkley Street. He spent his days slaving over a hot stove and his nights at his messy desk poring over paperwork and bills – probably as a way of easing the pain of losing Lola's mother.

David had suggested that Lola do a cooking course or get an apprenticeship, but the last thing she wanted to do was spend her evenings in a kitchen. Why should she, when there were tables to be danced on and pretty cupcakes to be made?

Besides, she couldn't really think about her father's suggestions for her future. She knew what she needed to do before she could figure out what to do with the rest of her life. In the meantime, she didn't have any real responsibility except to help out in the cafe as a waitress and have fun with her friends. And that was fine by her.

'I'm only eighteen, Dad — I've just finished school. I don't need to be so serious,' she had told him the last time he'd brought up the subject. It was easier to avoid the topic than tell her dad what she was really planning.

Lola untied her white apron and hung it on the wooden hook by the back stairs.

'I have to go and make myself look pretty,' she said, giving her dad a cheeky smile as she pulled at her bun, letting her dark red curls fall down her back.

David smiled and rolled his eyes as she ran up the stairs, two at a time, to the apartment above the cafe.

Turning on the shower, Lola stepped out of her sundress and looked at herself in the mirror. She had a smudge of ganache on her cheek and a sprinkling of the edible gold dust on her freckled nose. She was a messy cook, much to her father's frustration. *Clean as you go*, he was always nagging when she was in the kitchen.

But Lola didn't like to clean as she went. She was a whirlwind of energy and ideas, and none of them included washing dishes. Lola created chaos wherever she went. It was her trademark — or so her babcia said to anyone who would listen.

Not that Lola cared what Babcia thought. She was an old woman; she didn't know what it was like to be young.

'Don't worry so much, Babcia. Dance like nobody's watching, sing like nobody's listening,' she would say, as she flew off to her next party or club or adventure.

Lola liked to party. She was known for her staying power on the dance floor and for the all-nighters she regularly pulled.

'Europe isn't ready for you,' her dad had said, possibly only half-joking, when she had told him she was going travelling.

'Dad, they've had thousands of years to get ready for me,' she said poking out her tongue. 'Maybe I'll marry Prince Harry.'

Her father had snorted with laughter. 'You have to be joking! Being a princess isn't a fantasy, Lola, it's a burden.'

After showering and drying herself, she dropped her towel on her bedroom floor and stepped into her underwear before pulling her party dress from the hanger in her wardrobe. A lilac, dip-dyed minidress with a tutu skirt and tiny frills all over the bodice. *It's the perfect party dress*, thought Lola happily. She slipped it over her head, looked at herself in the mirror and clapped her hands.

'You look like vun of your cupcakes,' she heard her grandmother's voice say from the doorway. With her heavy Polish accent, Babcia sounded like a villain from a spy movie.

'Hi, Babcia,' said Lola, not turning around as she slid her feet into precariously high heels and fixed some tiny seed pearl earrings in her earlobes.

She put on some tinted moisturiser before dusting some pink

blush on her cheeks, tracing a lilac glitter eyeliner around her brown eyes and brushing on two coats of indigo blue mascara.

'Your father is stuffing chickens,' said Babcia, picking up Lola's towel from the floor.

'I know,' replied Lola as she sprayed herself with Baby Doll perfume. 'But I don't stuff anything except my face.'

The joke was clearly lost on Babcia, who was studying Lola's new backpack. It was sitting on her bed, overflowing with clothes.

Babcia sighed. 'That pack's not big enough. You should take a suitcase . . . on veals?'

Lola giggled, imagining her suitcase being carried across Europe by little calves. Babcia was seventy, very Polish and very old-fashioned – except, it seemed, when it came to suitcases on wheels. Babcia didn't understand why Lola would want to travel, not when she had a family business she could work in forever. To Babcia, family was everything.

Babcia was the mother Lola didn't have growing up, and had used a heavy dose of grandmotherly wisdom and Polish superstition to keep Lola in check. But as soon as Lola had booked her ticket to London, the apron strings were cut – at least from Lola's perspective.

'You have a jacket?' asked Babcia, looking disapprovingly at Lola's bare arms.

'No Babcia, I'm fine,' said Lola impatiently.

She never wore enough layers, according to her grandmother. She also wore her skirts too short and didn't have enough direction in life and should either stay working at the cafe or be at university. Certainly not running away from her family. And her hair was too red – although Lola could hardly help that. It was inherited from her mother.

Babcia sighed again, letting Lola know she was disappointed in her only grandchild, so Lola kissed her wrinkly cheek to show she appreciated the concern.

'Your guests vill be here soon,' said Babcia, her face softening slightly from the kiss. She glanced at herself in the mirror, patting her grey hair, which had been styled for the evening.

'I know, I'm going to set the table now,' said Lola, picking up the large shopping bag of decorations. 'Want to help?'

Babcia shrugged nonchalantly, but Lola knew her grandmother liked nothing more than to be needed.

'Okay, if you vant.'

'I vant,' said Lola as they clattered down the stairs together.

Cafe Ambrosia had once been a terrace house in a little inner-city street, but David had bought it and turned the ground floor into a cafe, with rooms upstairs for him, his beautiful young wife and baby Lola. He had kept the lovely Victorian features but opened the rooms downstairs into one large space, with a kitchen out the back. There was a small courtyard, but it was filled with boxes and milk crates. It had always been David's intention to turn it into a summer spot for customers to read the paper or let their little children play, but he hadn't got around to making it happen, even after all these years.

In the early days Babcia had worked in the kitchen, when she wasn't minding Lola, but her knees had started to hurt and she didn't understand the organic, soy, gluten-free revolution in the food industry, no matter how much her son explained it to her. So instead she devoted herself to the Polish Club, her garden and worrying about Lola.

'We'll eat here,' said Lola, gesturing to the large communal table, big enough to seat twelve comfortably.

Babcia wiped the already-clean table with lemon spray and Lola set out the cutlery and the place cards.

'Ben next to Rebecca,' she said aloud, as she carefully placed the handwritten cards on the table. 'Sarah next to Rosie. You next to Dad, of course.'

'Vhy you vant people to sit vhere you say? They can decide who they vant to talk to,' said Babcia as she picked up the card with her name.

'Babcia, let me be,' said Lola, trying to control her frustration. 'I vant it how I vant it, okay?'

Babcia was silent as she worked and Lola felt bad as she circled the table, laying out the cutlery. She knew she should be gentle with Babcia, but it was so hard.

For six months it had been like this, Babcia finding every little thing Lola did to be unsatisfactory. Lola knew that Babcia was upset about her leaving, but, seriously, everyone left home eventually.

The delicious smell of roasting chickens and garlic potatoes drifted from the kitchen and Lola's mouth watered. Her dad was also doing his feta and bean salad, and his roasted vegetable salad.

It was all Lola's favourite comfort food. Then there would be three types of dessert – the best part of any meal, in Lola's opinion. The gold-dusted chocolate cake with Chantilly cream on the side, a summer pudding, and cupcakes for those who wanted just a little something with their coffee.

Babcia was sweeping the floor as Lola lit tea-light candles and placed them in pink paper bags around the walls and on the windowsill. When she was satisfied that she was finished, she turned off the overhead lights and the room glowed.

'It looks pretty,' admitted Babcia.

In the soft light, Lola could see her grandmother's eyes were filled with tears. They gazed at each other for a long moment.

'My father used to say to me, *Stand still and vhat you seek vill come and find you.*' Babcia paused. 'You know, you don't have to travel to find the people who love you,' she finished, straightening the cutlery and blinking away her tears.

'That's not why I'm going, Babcia,' Lola said gently, putting her arms around the woman she loved most in the world. She got ready with her favourite half-lie. 'I'm going because I want to see the world.'

'The vorld isn't so amazing,' said Babcia with a sniff. 'It's nice here too.'

Lola laughed. 'I know, but seriously, you have to let it go, Babcia. Tomorrow I fly out of here. It doesn't mean I won't come back, though. I will, I promise.' Lola was in safe territory there – no half-lies in saying she was coming back.

Babcia reached out and held Lola's face in her hands. Then she said what she and Lola both knew. 'You vill look for her.'

Lola stood still, her brown eyes blinking as Babcia's faded blue eyes held hers. Just one more day of lying. 'I won't, I swear. I don't even care. I'm going for me, not for her.'

Babcia closed her eyes for a second, obviously not believing Lola. She murmured, like she often had over the years. 'She never came back.'

David appeared in the doorway of the kitchen.

'It looks beautiful, Lola,' he said proudly.

'Thanks, Dad.'

Lola pushed her grandmother's words out of her head for the moment. She went and took the tea towel from over her father's shoulder.

'Go and shower, you smell like garlic,' she said, pushing him towards the stairs.

'I always smell of garlic,' he said with a shrug.

The cafe door opened and Lola's best friends, Sarah and Rosie, walked in, both wearing pink feather boas.

'Oh my god,' squealed Lola, 'I want one!' Feathers flew into her mouth as she hugged her friends.

'And so it shall be, Lady Lola,' said Rosie dramatically as she pulled another pink boa out from behind her back and wrapped it around Lola's neck.

Lola held her friends in a group hug, feeling the tears prick at her eyes. 'God, I'm going to miss you both so much.'

'I'll be over in June,' Sarah reminded her. 'It's only four months away.'

Rosie pouted. 'While I'm stuck here going to lectures! I should have taken a year off like you two.'

Rosie was about to start a nursing degree and Sarah had put off her teaching degree for a year. Lola, however, hadn't committed to any university course. She honestly didn't know what she wanted to do after her trip. While she had enjoyed school because of her friends, she'd hated the work. She'd barely passed the final exams, but not because she was stupid. She just wasn't interested in anything school offered her.

The only subjects she'd excelled at were home economics and art. The cooking was easy; her final assessment was on cake decoration. Her art submission was a series of photographs of Barbie as famous masterpieces, such as the Mona Lisa and Venus de Milo. She'd received full marks and her work was included in the final year art exhibition at the state gallery. It was reviewed as being deeply ironic and part of a new generation of feminist art — not that Lola had tried to create a controversy. She genuinely loved both Barbie and photography. It seemed the perfect blend of her interests. The fact that her work was seen as important made Lola laugh.

'Drink?' Lola heard, and was relieved to turn and see her father, showered and fresh, handing out drinks.

Soon the rest of the guests arrived. A few of her father's friends, the ones who had rallied around them when things were tough, and a few of Babcia's friends from the Polish Club who had watched Lola grow up rounded out the guest list.

Lola looked at the familiar, loved faces around the table. These people were her family, but there was always one face missing — the face she was off to find. It sounded old-fashioned, but Lola couldn't help thinking that a real family had a mother and father, not just a crazy grandmother and a workaholic father — even though she loved them to bits.

It was time Lola found the woman who, eighteen years ago, had left her baby daughter next to the postbox without even a goodbye, never to return.

Until she found her, Lola knew her family would never be complete.

2

Viola Fair Batko had been born just before midnight, under an August full moon.

When they came home from hospital, apparently Lola cried. And cried and cried. She cried all the time. Her dad said Lola had been a colicky baby, whatever that meant. All Lola knew was that she cried too much.

Babcia always said it was because Lola's mum wouldn't let her tie a red ribbon around Lola's wrist. As punishment, bad spirits had come to rest in her cradle.

Hearing this story growing up, Lola had never been sure if the spirits had squatted in her cradle to punish her for crying so much, or if her mum was punished with a crying child because she didn't put a ribbon on Lola's wrist in the first place. Either way, they both ended up the losers.

Babcia's theory was that most things could be solved with a red ribbon. And everything that couldn't be solved that way could be fixed with a swim in the ocean. No matter the weather, or the time of day, Babcia claimed a swim in the sea would cure you of all moods and ills.

But her mum had never wanted to swim with Babcia. Apparently she had spent her days alone, looking after Lola in a half-hearted sort of way. She hardly ever went out. Babcia had stormed in one day and demanded David take control of his wife and baby.

It was pretty obvious to Lola that Babcia never approved of her parents' hasty marriage when her mum fell pregnant. Vivian wasn't Polish, she was too young to have children and she didn't want David to work nights when she had the baby. A chef, not working nights?

Finally, one day Vivian took Lola for a walk in the pram. No-one knew exactly what happened, but Lola had been told that her mother walked down to the corner and then got on a bus, leaving Lola in her pram by the red postbox.

It was Delia Grant, the traffic-crossing lady, who found Lola. She knew the baby with red hair and clenched fists, and returned her to David.

So Babcia had stepped in and helped out with Lola. They thought it would just be for a little while, but it had turned into

Lola's whole life. They never heard from Vivian again — all they knew was that she had gone to London.

As soon as Lola could understand that other little girls had mothers who loved them, she'd known it was her fault for driving her mother onto that bus and out of their lives. If she hadn't cried so much, if she hadn't been such an awful baby, then her mum might have stayed. They might have been a normal family.

In spite of this, Lola chose to be happy. Or at least, to appear that way. Whether it was boy troubles, money troubles or hair troubles, none of it mattered that much. If you took things too seriously, then you might just get onto a bus to nowhere.

David had tried his best to be both a mother and father to Lola. When she got her first period and had no mother to talk to, he'd bought every sort of sanitary pad and tampon on the market and placed them strategically around the house. Once, Lola even found some applicator tampons in the coolroom. She knew he was only trying to help, but he was just so clumsy with girl stuff. And who wanted to talk to their dad about their period?

Babcia wasn't about to explain the mysteries of messy first periods and messy first kisses, let alone contraception. So Lola had navigated her teens by herself, and mostly she did okay, except when she would lie in bed at night and wonder about her mum, and whether she missed her daughter.

There were baby photos from those three months when Vivian was in Lola's life. Lola always thought her mother — beautiful, with green eyes and a sad sort of smile — looked tired and really,

really young. She had the same red hair that refused to obey Lola's hairbrush.

As a child, information about her mum was hard to come by. Lola realised early on that her questions upset her father more than any tantrum could. He'd try to distract Lola with a chocolate treat, and eventually boxed up all the things that reminded him of Vivian and put them in the upstairs cupboard.

Babcia was bitter and judgemental when Lola asked her for details about her missing mother. 'Who leaves their own baby?' Babcia would mutter under her breath. 'And ven she's so tiny!' Then she'd launch into a stream of Polish curses and prayers all mixed together.

Lola kept the photographs of her mother, which she'd rescued from the upstairs cupboard, beside her bed, but she didn't even need to look at them anymore. She had burnt them into her memory, just in case her mum ever returned and she ran into her on the street. For as long as Lola could remember, she had studied every red-headed woman who walked into the cafe. And she still took a second glance when she passed other redheads in public.

So of course Babcia knew that Lola would be searching for her mum in London. And Lola knew that somehow, underneath the brittle layer of her powder and hairspray, Babcia understood. That's why Babcia hadn't said anything to her son about Lola's plans.

After the party, when the cafe floor was sticky with spilt drinks and scuffed from the dancing to Lola's 'party' playlist, Lola cleared the table with her father and set things as right as possible for the morning shift. She climbed the stairs, brushed her teeth and fell into bed without bothering to wash her face. It was nearly four in the morning, but she couldn't sleep, thinking about what was to come.

As a child, Lola had wished she could just close her eyes and wake up wherever her mother was. There was always a reasonable explanation for why her mum hadn't come back: she'd got amnesia or had been kidnapped. But she still desperately loved her long-lost daughter.

Lola closed her eyes now, and her mother's face came into her mind. *Will she know me?* Lola wondered. But how could she not know her? They were almost twins. Curvy, with small waists, crazy hair and heart-shaped faces. The only thing that Lola had inherited from her father was her brown eyes.

Babcia said Vivian's green eyes had been David's undoing. And perhaps they were. In the spirit of Babcia's crazy superstitions, Lola had long ago decided to stay away from any boy with green eyes. *Green eyes give out the evil eye, the curse of bad luck*, Babcia said. So Lola only dated boys with brown eyes. She would have happily dated ones with blue eyes, but none that Lola liked had shown up.

There had been plenty of casual boyfriends. She had slept with two boys: one to rid herself of her virginity when she was sixteen, and then her on-and-off-again boyfriend, Toby. He was a year older than her, and had headed up north the year before to work. They had parted on good terms, inasmuch as they were friends on Facebook — in fact, she'd seen an update recently that he was back in town. He was a nice guy, sweet and kind, but he wasn't someone she could imagine being with forever.

Not that Lola honestly gave boys much thought. Her friends were always scheming to make this or that boy like them, but Lola just didn't care that much. Instead, she spent her time scheming to get to London to find her mother.

Now that the time had finally come, Lola felt a wave of nerves and doubt. But, she reminded herself, her dad needed to go back to having his own life. And Babcia needed to worry about other people's red ribbons and bad-luck spirits for a while. And tend to her tomatoes.

If Lola went away, then maybe life could return to normal for them. She knew what a huge sacrifice her father had made for her. He hadn't had a real girlfriend since her mum had left. He'd had the occasional date, but only when Lola began to chastise him about getting out more.

But because they couldn't contact Lola's mum, her dad couldn't get a divorce. Well, he could, but it was difficult, and required him to dredge up painful memories. So he was still married to a woman he hadn't seen or heard from in eighteen years. And he pretty much refused to be with anyone else.

As always happened late at night, when Lola was thinking about all this, her sadness turned to anger. *Everyone's lives stopped while Mum went on to live hers, in London or wherever the heck she is*, thought Lola as she finally drifted off to sleep.

When Lola woke early in the morning, her mouth was dry and her head was host to a champagne-induced headache. She drank three glasses of water, took two aspirins, showered, dressed and went downstairs to the hum of the cafe.

Kelsey was working in the kitchen, assembling scrambled eggs on toast, and Fiona waved at her from the coffee machine. Both girls were backpackers from the UK who couldn't understand why Lola would want to go there.

'There's no work there,' Fiona had said in her Scottish accent.

'And London's big and lonely,' warned Kelsey.

But Lola had ignored them, just as she had ignored Babcia.

Wordlessly, Fiona handed Lola a strong latte with one sugar. Lola sipped it, feeling her body respond to the caffeine hit.

'Where's Dad?' she asked, poking her head through the servery window and smiling at Sanjay, who washed their dishes whenever he wasn't at university studying physics.

'He's gone to the market while we're quiet,' said Kelsey. 'We're out of basil.'

'What time are you leaving?' asked Fiona.

'Flight leaves at ten tonight,' Lola said as she grabbed a croissant from the basket on the counter.

Lola looked around the cafe that had been her playground as a child. The wooden floors were worn and the chairs were mismatched – not in a cool way. And Lola knew the walls needed a coat of paint. But at this moment, with people chatting and the familiar smells from the kitchen and the sound of the coffee machine hissing, Lola thought Cafe Ambrosia was just perfect.

The cafe was the only one for four blocks so, as her dad always said, they owned the coffee industry — at least, for four blocks they did. There had been a florist nearby, but that had been empty for a few months and now the windows were covered with paper.

There'd been a newsagency and a children's clothes shop, and an organic grocery. But they'd all closed over the years. Only an antiques shop, open odd hours, had survived. The shop was run by an old man Babcia had always told Lola to avoid, without ever explaining why. Over the years Lola had made up a series of stories about the man, ranging from him being a child stealer to a war criminal living in hiding. The shop always had ornate and bizarre window displays that fascinated her — or maybe it was the mystery that made the shop so intriguing.

As long as she could remember, Lola had crossed to the other side of Berkley Street whenever she saw the old man arranging his eclectic display of furniture at the front of his shop.

He used to watch her when she walked past and, as a child, she thought his interest was creepy and unsettling. But as she got older, she started to think that he really didn't look very sinister at all. And just last week he'd even raised his hand in a small wave as she passed by on the other side of the street. It was almost imperceptible, just enough for Lola to feel she should return it with a polite nod of her head.

It was a sort of acknowledgement, perhaps, but of what exactly? Lola wasn't sure. *This is exactly the sort of thing a girl would ask her mum*, she'd thought at the time.

If she wasn't going away she might have found the antique-shop mystery too compelling to not solve. But Babcia's distrust of an old guy who ran a dusty second-hand shop was hardly going to keep her awake when she was in London.

'Excuse me?' said a female voice, interrupting her thoughts.

Lola looked up to see a middle-aged blonde woman wearing what might have been the world's ugliest jumper.

'Hi there,' said Lola with a smile. She tried not to stare at the appliquéd bear ice-skating across the woman's jumper, surrounded by glitter snowflakes.

'I need to pay for my breakfast,' said the ice-skating bear's owner.

'No problem. Where were you sitting?' asked Lola, moving instantly into cafe mode.

'By the window,' the woman said shyly.

Lola gave her a reassuring smile, noticing as she went through the bills and found the order that she was quite a beautiful woman, apart from the jumper.

'Is it your dad who runs the cafe?' the woman tried to ask casually, but Lola could see she was blushing.

'It is,' said Lola, trying not to let her smile show. So many women had crushes on her dad; the skating bear lady was just another in a long line. 'Bircher muesli, raisin toast and a latte?

That's eighteen dollars fifty,' Lola said, ringing it up on the till. 'Your top is fun,' she added, as the woman handed her a twenty-dollar note.

'I know it's daggy,' replied the woman, taking her change and dropping it into the tip jar by the croissants, 'but my mum gave it to me and you know how you have to wear what your mum gives you. Well, at least once.'

'Are you seeing your mum today?' asked Lola. She always found other people's relationships with their mothers fascinating. How often did they see them, if they didn't live with them? Did they ring and ask for advice all the time, or just when things were really terrible? Did they really wear ugly jumpers just to please them?

'No, she lives in Queensland. I've just moved down here,' said the woman. She gestured around the cafe. 'I'm so glad I've found your cafe, it's lovely. It makes me feel almost cool — except for the jumper.' She gave a little laugh and Lola grinned. 'Anyway,' the woman continued, gathering up her wallet and putting it back in her bag, 'I'll see you again tomorrow.'

'Oh no, you won't. I'm leaving for overseas. Tonight!' Excitement bubbled up inside Lola.

'Oh, how exciting. Where are you going?'

'London first. And then, who knows!'

'Are you going with anyone? Or meeting anyone there?'

Lola looked around and saw that no-one was listening other than this lovely woman — and perhaps the ice-skating bear.

'I'm going to find my mother,' she whispered. 'She lives in London.'

This woman would probably be the last person Lola would serve at Cafe Ambrosia, and she wanted to remember her. Lola looked at the woman's face. She was pretty sure she'd remember the bear jumper, so she focused on committing her pretty, open face to memory instead.

Lola had no idea why she told a stranger about her mother. Maybe saying it out loud would make it more real, she thought, as she made her way upstairs to finish packing. She hadn't told anyone until now, not her besties, not Babcia, and certainly not her dad. But she figured as long as the bear and its owner could keep their mouths shut, her secret would be safe.

3

Lola had fallen asleep in the middle of repacking her backpack. She woke to the sound of the phone in the apartment ringing. Wiping the dribble from her cheek and checking her mobile, she saw it was nearly midday.

Still plenty of time to get organised, she thought, and let the phone go through to the answering machine. No-one interesting ever called the landline.

She stretched and ran through the list of things she still had to do. Pack toothbrush, charge phone, don't forget phone and charger. Oh, and the adaptor thingy for the electrical sockets—

She could hear a voice in the other room, coming through the speaker of the answering machine.

'Hello, this is Di Mills from Alfred Hospital Emergency. Could Viola Batko please call me back as soon as possible? I'm afraid it's urgent. The number here is —'

Babcia, Lola thought in a panic as she hurdled the coffee table to pick up the handset. Her heart was beating fast. 'This is Viola Batko,' she said, rubbing her knee where it had hit the edge of the table.

'Hi Viola.' The woman paused as though preparing someone for something. That pause made Lola's heart beat even faster. 'Your father, David, has been brought in to us at Emergency. He's had an accident.'

Lola sat down on the coffee table, the pain in her knee forgotten. 'What sort of accident?' she asked quickly, and probably too loudly. She didn't know whether to be relieved it wasn't Babcia or worried it might be worse. 'Is he okay?'

'It's probably best if you come down to the hospital,' said the woman in a maddeningly calm voice. 'Are you far away?'

Lola felt her stomach clench with fear. 'Is he okay?' she asked again.

The nurse paused. 'He's stable for now, but he has suffered a major trauma, so it would be best for you to come in as soon as you can.'

'I'm on my way,' Lola said.

She hung up the phone, slipped on her shoes and grabbed her purse and mobile. She was clattering down the stairs when her mobile rang and she saw Babcia's number come up on the screen.

'Babcia, did they call you as well?' she asked as she debated whether to call a taxi or try to hail one on the street. The idea of waiting for anything made her feel even more panicked, so she ran through the cafe, not speaking to anyone, and out onto the street.

'Did who call me?' asked Babcia.

Lola cursed herself for not having her driver's licence yet. She wished more than anything she had been a proper grown-up and got her licence when she'd turned eighteen.

'It's Dad,' said Lola, knowing she should control the panic in her voice like the nurse had, but not quite managing to. She waved at a cab up ahead, and sprinted to where it had pulled over. 'He's in hospital. There was an accident, but I don't know anything else. I'm on my way now.'

Babcia let out a long string of emotional Polish that Lola didn't fully understand. She also cursed herself for not learning more Polish. Babcia had often tried to teach her, but the words just didn't stick. Lola had always said she would never need it because didn't plan on going to Poland.

'Babcia, I can't understand you,' said Lola as she climbed into the back seat of the taxi. To the driver, she said, 'The Alfred Hospital.'

'I'm coming,' said Babcia, and she hung up.

Lola sat in the back seat, looking at her phone. Who should she call? Maybe she shouldn't call anyone until she knew more. God, she didn't know what you were supposed to do at a time like this.

After the longest fifteen minutes of her life, the taxi pulled up outside the hospital. Lola paid and ran inside.

'I'm here to see David Batko,' she said breathlessly to the woman at the front desk. The woman, obviously used to frantic relatives, smiled reassuringly at Lola as she searched on the computer.

'Take a seat and someone will be with you soon,' she said, gesturing at the row of plastic chairs. Lola was sure a concerned look had passed over the woman's face, but she tried to tell herself she was being paranoid.

Lola perched on the edge of the nearest seat. *Please let him be okay. Please let him be okay. Please let him be okay.* She rocked back and forth slightly, part of her knowing she probably looked crazy, part of her thinking it would somehow help her dad be okay.

'Viola Batko?' she heard. She looked up to see a woman in green scrubs, red crocs and clear plastic—framed glasses pushing back her hair.

'Yes,' she said, standing up. The woman introduced herself to Lola, but Lola immediately forgot her name and everything she said about her role at the hospital.

'Come through.'

Lola followed the woman through some automatic doors marked 'Staff Only' in red letters. The sound of machines beeping and people murmuring filled Lola's head as they walked through another door and down a corridor. Something about the way the woman was leading her through the hospital made all the questions on her lips dry up. Next thing she knew, Lola was following the woman into a room. She expected to see her father in a white gown in a hospital bed. Instead, it was a room devoid of anything but a box of tissues and two sofas facing each other.

Lola instinctively knew it was the room where the bad news was delivered. *Oh god, oh god, oh god*, she thought as she sat down on the couch opposite the woman.

A man in the same green scrubs came in and joined them on the couches.

The woman spoke again. 'As I explained, I'm the doctor looking after your dad. This is Steve, he's one of the nurses here.'

'What's going on?' said Lola, the fear making her sound angry. 'No-one's told me anything.'

'Your dad's been hit by a car,' said the doctor in a calm voice.

Lola swallowed and blinked a few times.

'He has a suspected head injury and broken pelvis.'

'Head injury?'

'Yes. But at this early stage we can't confirm the extent of the damage. It may be very minor, or it could be quite serious. We won't know until we've done some tests. He's having an MRI as we speak.'

Why did her dad go to the stupid market? He could have sent Fiona or Kelsey! Why couldn't this be happening to someone else's dad? Her head was full of awful, angry, worried thoughts. *He never asks anyone to do anything,* she thought angrily. *And now this!*

'Can I see him?'

The doctor looked at Steve, who nodded. 'He's probably back from his MRI, so give us a minute and we'll get him ready for you.'

The stood up and left Lola alone.

Lola was starting to feel hysterical. How would they *get him ready*? Shave him? Brush his hair? Mop up the blood? She looked down to see that she had grabbed a tissue and was ripping it into tiny little pieces.

Lola sank back into the seat and closed her eyes. *Don't die, Daddy*, she prayed. It was a long time since she'd called her dad 'Daddy'. *This is because I was going off to look for Mum. This is all my fault. The universe knew and now I'm being punished.*

Lola felt the tears falling and reached for another tissue. *Lola, stop it, stay focused. You're turning into Babcia with your stupid superstitions.* She wiped her eyes and blew her nose. The tissues were the good ones, thick and soft. No expense spared for the worst of times.

You have to be an adult, she told herself, looking up as Steve opened the door. 'He's ready.'

For what? thought Lola, as though in a dream. *His close-up? His last rites?* 'Lola, get it together,' she muttered aloud.

'Pardon?' asked the nurse.

'Nothing,' she said as she followed him down yet another corridor and around the corner.

Lola followed Steve into a cubicle, her arms folded across her chest as though that might protect her from what lay behind the curtains. Steve drew the curtain aside. Her father was lying on a bed. He was drawn and pale and asleep.

'He's in an induced coma,' said the nurse. 'His breathing is still irregular so we're monitoring that closely.' He checked a drip in her dad's wrist.

Lola felt like throwing up.

'David, your daughter Viola is here,' said Steve with forced brightness.

'Lola,' she said. 'It's just Lola.'

She stepped forward and took her father's hand. The one without the drip. She didn't know why she bothered to correct him, but it felt important. Viola had always felt too serious for her. It was the name of the heroine in a Shakespeare play. Apparently her mother had loved *Twelfth Night*.

'Hi Daddy,' she said, her voice catching.

'David. *O moj Boze!*'

Lola heard Babcia's voice behind her and turned to see her grandmother, pale with shock, holding on to the flimsy blue curtain for support. Lola's heart nearly broke at the sight of her formidable babcia looking so crushed. She reached out to Babcia and pulled her into a fierce hug before leading her closer to the hospital bed. The nurse pushed a plastic chair towards Lola, who eased her grandmother into it.

'He's got a head injury and a broken pelvis,' she said gently to Babcia, who gasped even though Lola was pretty sure she didn't really understand what any of it meant. Not that Lola did herself.

'We have to wait for some test results before we know how bad it is.'

Lola stroked her father's thinning brown hair, noticing the slight stubble on his chin. He looked tired and drawn in the harsh light – or did he always look like that? When was the last time she actually stopped and looked at her father? She was always rushing around; they never sat and really talked. And now, this. It was her fault for having such a late night and making him so tired that he'd walk in front of a car while crossing the road to buy some stupid basil.

Babcia started to pray as she wound a red ribbon around her son's wrist. Lola dashed away tears as the doctor walked into the cubicle, looking down at her clipboard.

'Okay, so we have the results back from the MRI.'

Lola held her breath and made a pact with God or whoever might be listening. *Please let him be okay, I won't go away, I won't look for Mum. I'll stay and be responsible and smart. I'll be the best daughter I can be.*

'The MRI shows he has bruising and swelling around the brain, but no bleeding.' She looked down at Lola and Babcia's worried faces. 'That's good,' she explained. 'We'll keep him in the coma until the swelling goes down, but it's highly unlikely he'll have any permanent brain damage.'

Thank you, Lola said silently, and she and Babcia fell into each other's arms in relief.

'The pelvis, however, is another matter,' said the doctor.

Lola pulled away from Babcia and looked up at the woman.

'It's shattered. He'll require surgery and intensive rehabilitation work before he can walk again. It's likely to take months. But the good news is he should regain full movement over time.'

Lola knew that was bad news, but knowing there was no brain damage was all she could really focus on.

'How long vill you keep him?' asked Babcia, looking at the doctor as though they were keeping her son prisoner rather than saving his life. She didn't trust doctors, since in her world there was nothing a swim or red ribbon wouldn't fix.

'Do you mean how long in the rehab centre, or how long in the hospital?' asked the doctor, either not noticing or choosing to ignore Babcia's rudeness.

'Both,' said Lola, before Babcia could say anything else to offend the doctor.

The doctor shrugged. 'I like to be conservative . . . ' she thought for a moment. 'I would say at least ten weeks, give or take a few.'

Lola nodded and looked down at her father. The love she felt for him was overwhelming, and she let the tears fall as she leant down and kissed his cool forehead.

'I love you, Dad,' she whispered in his ear. 'Even if you don't look when you cross the road.'

The doctor smiled sympathetically at Lola, then said, 'I'll give you three some privacy.' She drew the curtain and left quietly.

Turning to Babcia, Lola straightened her shoulders and swept her long hair up into a high bun. 'He's going to be okay, Babcia,' she said, allowing herself to believe it.

Babcia searched Lola's face for hope, her face ashen.

'He is,' said Lola firmly, as though she had spoken with the big man himself and she knew the way the cards were going to fall. 'Here's what's going to happen,' she said in a serious voice she didn't even know she owned. 'I'm going to go back to the cafe and make sure everything's okay there.'

Babcia nodded.

'You'll stay here for a while, and when I get back later we'll organise everything. Okay?'

Babcia nodded again. She looked like she'd aged ten years in the last few minutes. 'You aren't going away then?' she asked quietly.

Lola paused as her mother's face flashed up in her mind. She forced a smile at her grandmother.

'No, Babcia, I'm here,' she said, and she squeezed her father's hand. She could have sworn she felt him squeeze it limply back in return. 'I'm not going anywhere,' she said to her silent father, and the now-weeping Babcia. 'I've totally got this covered. Don't worry about anything.'

But of course she was worried. About her dad, about Babcia — and about how on earth she was going to keep running the cafe.

And she was worried about whether she'd ever get the chance to find her mum.

4

Lola arrived back at the cafe to find Kelsey and Fiona stressed and overworked, trying to run the kitchen and keep things going on the cafe floor. Sanjay had abandoned the dishes and was cooking omelettes – the only thing he knew how to cook – for hungry customers.

'Faaaark,' said Fiona when she saw Lola walk through the door. 'What's going on? Where's David?'

Lola pulled Fiona and Kelsey into the kitchen. Sanjay, seeing the look on Lola's face, took a pan off the heat and joined them.

'Dad's been hit by a car,' Lola told the three of them, pausing to allow the news to sink in.

'Jesus,' said Kelsey.

'How bad is it?' asked Sanjay, his face crumbling.

Everyone loved David. He was a father figure to everyone who worked in the cafe. In the past fifteen years he had given three waitresses away at their weddings, and was known to give advances on pay cheques, invaluable advice, and free meals to the homeless, lost and lonely.

'It could've been much worse. He has swelling around his brain, but no bleeding, so that's good news. I guess. But he has a broken pelvis. He's in an induced coma until the swelling goes down.'

Lola tried to sound positive but she felt a wave of tiredness as she spoke. She glanced through the servery window and saw all the people in the cafe, two of them lined up to pay, adding to her sense of being overwhelmed.

'So, he'll be okay?' prompted Fiona.

'I think so, but he's going to be out of action for at least two months.' Lola rubbed her temples.

'What can we do?' asked Sanjay.

Lola felt her eyes fill with tears at his question. 'I don't know, Sanjay. I don't know how I'm going to run this place. I can only bake cakes, which isn't going to keep a cafe going. And we can't exactly afford to pay for a proper chef to take over.'

'I can cook a few dishes,' said Kelsey, but she sounded defeated already.

'I know, but we need a real cook. Sorry,' said Lola, gently.

Kelsey reached out and rubbed Lola's arm sympathetically.

Fiona went and served the customers waiting to pay, and then came back into the kitchen.

'I know a guy here, from London,' she said suddenly, like the thought had just struck her. 'Sam. He's staying down at the hostel. He's a cook back home. He's backpacking around Australia, but he might do a few shifts for cash, till you get yourself sorted at least.'

'Could you ask him?' asked Lola, relieved to have at least one option.

'Yep,' said Fiona.

'Um . . . now?' asked Lola as she looked through the servery window and saw three customers walk out after seeing the sign that had been crudely stuck to the front of the till that read, 'Omelettes and scrambled eggs only for lunch'.

'Okay. If he's not there I'll leave a message,' said Fiona. Untying her apron, she grabbed her bag and her bike helmet and hurried out the back to where her bike was chained up.

The others got back to work. Lola walked into the coolroom and closed the door. She turned a milk crate upside down, sat on it and put her head in her hands. What the hell was she going to do now? She sat in the cold silence, trying to get her head around everything that had happened. Would Dad really be okay? Would he be able to walk? What if he was brain damaged, even just a little bit? *God help him*, she thought as she went through the possible outcomes. She didn't know how long she was sitting there, thinking and stressing, before she was startled by someone pulling open the coolroom door.

Kelsey's head popped in. 'You okay? You've been in there for half an hour, you know. You'll get a cold.'

'I'm okay,' Lola lied.

'Your friends are here to see you.'

Lola took a deep breath and walked out to the cafe, where Rosie and Sarah were smiling and waving little Union Jack flags at her. Their cheery ignorance of what had happened that morning was like a stab to Lola's heart.

'Toodle-oo, pip pip,' said Sarah.

'Cheerio, cor blimey,' said Rosie, giggling. 'Have a cuppa char and chip buttie,' she added in an appalling English accent.

Sarah started to laugh. 'And then put your toad in my hole and show me your spotted dick!'

They doubled over, cracking themselves up. Lola stood watching them, hardly knowing how to form the words to explain what was going on. Sanjay, who was wiping down tables, gave Lola a sympathetic look.

Just then Fiona walked back through the door.

Lola turned from the girls and looked at Fiona, who nodded towards the door. Standing in the doorway was a very cute guy in shorts, boots and a worn white T-shirt. He wasn't tall, but then he wasn't short either. He had light brown hair and stubble on his face. His wrists were covered with lengths of plaited leather.

Oh Christ, a hippie, thought Lola. *He'll want to serve lentils and then he'll make hash cookies and the customers will get stoned and we'll end up on some current affairs show.*

'Lola, this is Sam,' said Fiona.

Rosie and Sarah had stopped laughing and were looking from Lola to this new guy in the doorway, aware now that something was going on.

'Hi, Lola,' Sam said with a smile that was both kind and comforting.

'Hi,' Lola said, encouraged by his smile. 'Fi, could you take Sam through to the kitchen? Just give me a moment.'

Fiona led Sam around the three girls and into the kitchen.

'What's going on?' asked Rosie.

'It's Dad. He's in hospital,' said Lola.

'Oh my god. What happened?'

'He was hit by a car. Broken pelvis, head injury, but he should be okay.' Lola realised she sounded like a robot when she gave the report.

Rosie and Sarah rushed forward to hug her.

'Shit,' said Sarah. 'What are you going to do? Should we go and have a drink or something? We can talk about it.'

Lola shook her head. 'I have to work things out for the cafe first. That's the most important thing.'

Rosie nodded. 'I guess you're not leaving tonight then?'

Lola frowned. 'Of course not.'

'We should leave you to sort this out then. If you don't need us? Call later, yeah? To let us know how he is?' Sarah squeezed Lola's hand.

Lola nodded and walked past Fiona, who was already back on

the coffee machine, and opened the door to the kitchen.

'Okay, sorry,' she said to Sam, who was leaning against the bench talking to Kelsey. 'It's all a bit of a drama.'

'I told him about your dad and the trip and everything,' said Fiona, sticking her head through the servery window.

Lola nodded, grateful that she didn't have to run through the medical report again. 'Are you a trained chef?' she asked Sam.

'Nope,' he said with a shrug. 'I just know how to cook.'

Underneath the surface friendliness he seemed careful and wary, thought Lola.

She looked at Fiona, who nodded. 'He's really good, Lola. Everyone at the hostel loves his food.'

'Can you work fast?' she asked him.

'I can,' he said simply, without any arrogance. That was a good sign, in Lola's books.

'How long could you stay for? Dad won't be home for weeks yet.' Her brain was working fast. She was thinking ahead for the first time in her life, and it felt weird.

'How long do you need me?' His accent was soft, slightly crisp but not too posh.

'I don't know,' said Lola honestly, as she wrung her hands. 'Two months, maybe more.'

The bell on the cafe door rang, and Fiona peered around Lola at Kelsey. 'Hey, can you please help me out here?' Kelsey nodded and left the kitchen, and Fiona left the servery window to greet the customers, leaving Lola and Sam alone.

Lola paused. 'I don't know how much I can pay you,' she admitted. 'It's not as though we're making a lot of money.' She gestured around the kitchen as if to prove her point.

Sam thought for a moment. 'You don't have a spare room, do you? You could pay me less if I had a room to stay in.'

'What?' Lola was startled. She needed a cook, not a flatmate.

'I need a room,' explained Sam. 'I'm going insane at the hostel. I'm sick of the stealing and the bullshit and the noise. I promise I'm not weird or messy or anything like that,' he said, with that winning smile again.

'Um, I'm just looking for a cook. Nothing else.' Lola felt uncomfortable with this turn of events, and found herself crossing her arms.

Sam nodded, blushing a little. It made him more likeable, less weird. 'Sure, I understand. Totally. Just asking.'

Lola glanced through the servery window and saw two more customers walk out, mumbling about the omelette situation. That was probably about forty dollars walking out the door.

'Wait here,' she said to Sam.

She walked out to where Fiona was cleaning a table. 'He wants to move in,' Lola said in a whisper.

'What?' Fiona looked up at Lola, a dishcloth in her hand.

'He said I could pay him less if he had a place to stay,' Lola hissed. 'Is he creepy or what?'

'Not that I know of,' said Fiona. 'He's a really nice guy. Everyone says so.'

Lola glanced back at the kitchen and then back to Fiona.

'Maybe I should do it. God knows today was a massive fail, we must have lost a lot of money.' She turned and walked back to the kitchen, thinking. Sam was reading the menu.

'You can have the job, but I'm not sure yet about the room,' she said carefully.

'That's great,' he said, then paused. 'So, what's the pay?'

'I don't know,' she admitted. 'What should you be paid?'

Sam laughed. 'Jesus, you're going to get fleeced if you go around asking people what they think they should be paid.'

Lola bristled. 'This is all new to me.' She looked at the clock on the wall. 'I was supposed to be flying to London tonight. On the trip of a lifetime. Instead, my dad's in hospital in a coma and won't be able to walk for weeks and I'm here trying to run a cafe for the first time in my life.'

'I'm sorry,' he said earnestly. 'I can't imagine what you're going through, but I do know it must be complete shite.' He ran his hand through his hair.

Lola appreciated his apology. 'Can I look at the books and see what I can afford?' She wondered where her father kept all the accounts. Was it in the big pile of papers upstairs?

Sam paused. 'You're in a right mess, aren't you?' His voice was gentle as he spoke, not mean or judgemental. It made Lola want to cry.

She nodded at him. 'Yep. I have no idea what I'm doing. Or how I'm going to cope.'

'But your dad's going to be alright?' Sam seemed concerned, even though he'd never met the guy.

'I think so. But he's going to take ages to get better. This is all Dad's domain,' Lola gestured around the kitchen. 'I just baked the cakes.'

'Are you a pastry chef?'

'Me? A chef? No way,' said Lola with a wry smile. 'I just like to bake. It's a good distraction.'

Sam nodded. 'I know what you mean.'

Lola sucked on her bottom lip and thought for a minute. 'You seem normal,' she said. 'What's your favourite film?'

'Huh?'

'Favourite film?' Lola persisted.

He thought for a minute, and she noticed he had really nice skin. Softer than the skin that Australian men had.

'*Fight Club* or *The Shawshank Redemption*,' he answered.

Lola rolled her eyes. 'What is it with guys and *The Shawshank Redemption*? Fave book?'

'*Fight Club*.'

'That's a movie.'

'First it was a book, by Chuck Palahniuk.'

Lola shrugged. 'Cool.' She thought for a moment. 'If you were on death row, what would your last meal be?'

It was Sam's turn to think for a moment. 'Steak, medium rare, pomme frites and a green salad, a bottle of Asahi and meringue with berries and cream to finish.'

'You mean a pavlova,' said Lola.

'You call it pavlova, I call it Eton mess. Either way, it's my comfort food.'

'Not chocolate?' asked Lola suspiciously. Didn't everyone love chocolate? She didn't trust people who said they didn't like chocolate.

'Maybe some chocolate shavings over the top, just to be entirely indulgent.'

Lola smiled. 'Okay, you can move in. But if it doesn't work, I will be upfront with you. Life's too short for bullshit.'

Sam nodded.

'And I warn you, I have a boyfriend,' lied Lola. 'So don't get all weird and creepy.'

'That's okay, I have a girlfriend too,' said Sam. 'So I'd appreciate if you didn't get all weird and creepy either.' He had a twinkle in his eye.

Lola laughed and felt a little relieved. Perhaps it would work out okay. She heard her phone ring and pulled it from her pocket. Unknown number.

'Hello?' she answered.

'Lola, it's Babcia.' Her voice was small and worried.

'Is everything all right?' Lola asked. 'Is it Dad?' Her heart was beating fast. She saw Sam look at her, concerned.

'He is still sleeping,' said Babcia. 'I vonder if you vill come and take me home.'

Lola looked at Sam and widened her eyes in frustration. For over half a century Babcia had been getting around the city by herself, using cabs and public transport. Now she needed a chaperone?

Lola was about to say as much, when a fog of guilt and sympathy enveloped her. 'Yes, I'll come and get you,' she said gently. 'I want to see Dad again anyway.'

She said goodbye, hung up and put the phone into her pocket. 'That was my grandma,' she explained to Sam. 'Old, Polish, a little bit crazy. Don't say I didn't warn you.' Her attempt at humour fell flat to her own ears, but Sam smiled.

'So, I need to go back to the hospital,' Lola said, wondering what decision she'd have to make next. There were so many decisions to make, it was doing her head in.

Sam made it easy for her. 'Why don't I work out what dishes I can make with the food we have for tomorrow, and then you and I can go through it all and get our ducks in a row first thing tomorrow?'

Lola could have kissed him. 'Thank you.'

'No problem.'

Sam walked towards the coolroom and opened the door. Lola stood watching him and realised she felt almost calm for the first time since that awful phone call.

'When will you move in?' she asked, pausing at the back door.

'Tonight too soon?' he asked. 'There are some Swedes in town for the Australian Open and they are so freaking loud with their chanting, I can't sleep.'

Yes, thought Lola, *tonight is too soon*. But a deal was a deal.

'Fine, you can have Dad's room,' she said crisply. 'It's upstairs. There's a spare key in the onion bin. Don't steal anything and don't go into my room, okay?'

'Okay.' Sam smiled and went into the coolroom as Lola slammed the back door behind her.

What have you done, Lola? she wondered as she rode the bus to the hospital. *You have just let a stranger take over where you live and work. Oh, you're an idiot sometimes.* She prayed to whoever the benevolent god of flatmates was to not let her be murdered in her sleep that night.

5

Sam sprinted back to the hostel as soon as he'd gone through the coolroom and figured out a bit of a plan for the next day's menu. He was so pleased to be out of Shithole Hostel, as he called it, that he did a little fist pump in the air before realising how stupid he must look to anyone passing him in the street.

The hostel was only ever meant to be for a few days, but days had turned into weeks and still Sam hadn't moved on. The truth was he liked the city more than he thought he would.

When he'd arrived from London he'd been mentally and emotionally exhausted, barely able to speak. The hostel had been ideal; nobody asked too many questions, and most people left him alone. He was just the quiet one who cooked great food.

Everyone was just passing through and partying hard along the way, generally making a lot of noise as they did so.

He knew that, in a way, he was just running away by going backpacking. But he couldn't stay home, in a city that constantly pushed him back into the past, reminding him of all that he'd lost. There were no reminders in this new city, no-one with concerned, pity-filled eyes, no hushed voices asking him how he was. But, as time had gone on at the hostel, he'd also realised there was no quiet, no unbroken sleep and no real privacy. It was time to move on.

Sam pushed open the hostel door and nodded at the girl at the desk.

'What's for tea, Sam?' she called in her thick Scottish accent.

'No idea, love,' he said with a smile as he ran up the stairs. 'I'm leaving!'

'What?' he heard her call behind him.

But he didn't stop to answer as he strode down the hallway to his room. He knew he'd come across as pushy when he'd asked the girl at the cafe for a room, but he needed a way to move on, move out. And he'd work for next to nothing to be away from the drunken backpackers.

Getting away from London had been a good idea, but he also needed to get some proper sleep. And he needed to put his soul into something.

He shoved his few belongings into his backpack and pulled the sheets off his bunk bed, putting them in the laundry basket in the hallway. He took one last look at the room where he had lived for over a month. *Goodbye bunk beds, goodbye window that doesn't open more than a centimetre, goodbye squeaky overhead fan, goodbye threadbare carpet.*

Sam swung his pack onto his back and walked down the hallway, past a girl on the smokers' balcony who was crying into her phone in Spanish.

'Adios,' he said under his breath as he ran down the stairs and out of the hostel. He had paid nearly a week ahead, but he didn't even care.

The problem with all the other backpackers at the hostel was that they were all embracing life, while Sam was running away from it. That mix was never going to work. Sam didn't want to drink or party, and he had no funny stories of his travels or wild adventures to boast about.

He could tell them a thing or two about grief though. That sometimes he lay in bed all day, wishing he could sleep away the hours. That, despite the infectious energy and bustle of the city, his favourite hangout was the end of the St Kilda pier, where he'd sat some nights so he could cry in peace.

No, these weren't the sort of stories you shared. He wasn't fun to be around, he knew that. But right now, on the walk back to the cafe, he felt almost happy. For pretty much the first time since it happened.

The little cafe seemed pleasant enough. Nothing like the last restaurant he'd worked at in London, but he didn't need that fancy stuff anymore. He just wanted to get back to what he loved: food.

There was something about taking the ingredients, which on their own seemed so humble, and then turning them into a meal that people would remember. That was what he loved about working in kitchens. If you took away all the hype, the reviews and the critics and the drama, there was just the food. If the food was great, then nothing else mattered.

Sam wanted to get back to the cafe before Lola returned. He needed to make this work. He suspected he was much too fucked up to work in a big kitchen again — for the time being, anyway. He needed to connect with cooking again, and the small kitchen of Cafe Ambrosia seemed like the perfect place to fall back in love.

Fiona and Kelsey were cleaning and packing up when he returned.

'Hey,' he said, closing the door behind him. He knew Fiona from the hostel, but only a little. She seemed pleasant enough.

Kelsey stood in the doorway of the kitchen and Fiona put her head through the servery window. They glared at him.

'So, you're moving in?' asked Fiona, looking at him suspiciously.

'Lola said it was okay,' said Sam, feeling the heat of her stare. 'That way I'll work for less money.'

'You better not get all rapey with her,' Kelsey said, her eyes narrowing.

'Oh my god,' said Sam, looking at her with his mouth agape.

'I'm just saying,' she said, and turned from him as she started to mop the floor.

'She's fine, I'm fine, it's all fine,' said Sam, dumping his backpack in the corner.

'And don't steal anything,' said Fiona.

'Jesus, you two are the trusting sort, aren't you?' Sam shook his head.

'Lola's dad, David, is the nicest guy in the world. Lola is cute but kind of young,' said Fiona. 'We just want to make sure she's okay.'

'I get it, and you're well within your rights to question my intentions,' said Sam easily. Hell, if it were his sister who had just allowed a stranger to move in, he would have had a blue fit.

'So what are they?' demanded Kelsey, following him into the kitchen.

'What? My intentions?'

'Yeah,' she said, but this time her voice was friendlier.

Sam paused. What were his intentions? He tried to remember. Wake up, breathe, shower, get through the day without crying, eat something delicious, smile, see the birds in the sky, look for signs from Katherine.

'I just want to cook,' he said, and smiled at her. 'And not sleep in a hostel for a while. At least until I decide where I will move on to next.'

This answer seemed to satisfy Kelsey and Fiona, who went on with their tasks.

A few minutes later, Fiona called through the servery window: 'We're off. Oh, the cafe opens at seven and closes at five.'

'All right then,' Sam said cheerfully, focusing more on his list than on saying goodbye.

'See you in the morning,' said Kelsey, in a way that made Sam think she didn't want to leave him there on his own.

He straightened up and looked at the girls as they headed outside. Sam could see them talking to each other out the front. *They needn't worry,* he thought. He had no designs other than being in the kitchen and sleeping in a decent bed.

Eventually curiosity got the better of him, and he headed up the stairs to the apartment. The door opened into a very comfortable room, with old furniture and a large sofa covered in brightly coloured cushions with pompoms around the trim. There was a TV, and one wall had a bookshelf filled with cookbooks. Sam thought he could have lived happily in that room forever. The Persian rug was worn, and a vintage coffee table sat in the centre of the room with a Lonely Planet guide to Great Britain and a print-out of a boarding pass on it.

He picked up the pass. *Viola Fair Batko,* he read. *Melbourne to London.*

Total shite thing to have happened, he thought, as he put the ticket down again. But then, life wasn't fair. He had learnt that in the worst way possible.

He walked down the hallway, where three doors faced him. The first door opened into the bathroom, with a skull-and-crossbones shower curtain that made him smile. He opened the next door, where a sea of pink assaulted him. Lola's room, obviously. From his vantage point in the doorway he could see two framed photos on the bedside table. One was Lola as a little girl, judging from the mad red hair and the fairy costume. The other was a woman with red hair and pretty smile, who he guessed was Lola's mother.

He risked crossing the room to look more closely at the pictures. He thought the mother's gaze looked a bit vacant, and he turned to the other photo, comparing them. Lola's face was filled with life, but the woman looked like she was in another world.

He quickly left the room, shutting the door carefully behind him. Lola had specifically told him not to go into her room.

He opened the third door, opposite Lola's, and saw a neatly made queen-sized bed. Under the window was a wooden bench. A red rug lay on the floor, and there was a stack of cookbooks and magazines by the bed. Sam dumped his backpack and sat down on the bed and listened. Silence. It was so long since he had heard silence. You needed silence, otherwise you forgot what your thoughts sounded like.

Sam didn't know what to do first: have a shower, have a sleep, or go back into the kitchen. But his work ethic got the better of him, and he stretched and headed downstairs.

The cafe was small, a little shabby but not enough to turn anyone away. Sam figured they probably served excellent coffee and reasonable cafe-standard food. Enough to make a living and pay the bills. Sam went through the menu again. He could make most of the things on it with his eyes closed, and what he couldn't make, he would substitute for something similar.

Sam felt more at peace than he had in a long time. Not that he wasn't still hurting. Perhaps what the priest had said afterwards was true: *No matter how fast you run, you can't outpace the sense of loss. It will catch up with you eventually, but that's okay. It's as it should be.*

Sam pulled out his phone and pressed a number.

'Hello, you've called Katherine, leave a message and I'll get back to you as soon as I can,' came her voice.

Sam paused, his eyes stinging from tears impatient to fall. It was still bittersweet to hear her voice, even a year later.

'Hey, babe,' he said, his voice cracking. 'I got a job. It's in a nice little cafe, and I have a room. No more Shithole Hostel for me. Anyway, thought you might want to know. Just keeping you up to date.' He paused. 'All right then, speak later, babe. I love you.' He shut off his phone and looked at the black screen.

One year on and he still called his dead girlfriend's phone? He still wanted to leave her messages about what he was doing and where he was? *I'm insane*, he thought, as he put the phone in his pocket and ran his hands through his hair.

'Fuck it,' he said aloud. He put his hands on the steel bench and looked at his distorted reflection in the dull metal.

He's too young to know grief, he had overheard his mother say at the funeral.

Twenty-one was also too young to get married, Katherine's mother had said at the time, but no-one mentioned that after what had happened.

Twenty-one was definitely too young to die. Everyone knew that Katherine, who was studying to be a physiotherapist, was clever. And everyone knew that Katherine was incredibly unlucky to have suffered a brain aneurysm. *Only the good die young*, they said. *They are arseholes, whoever they are,* thought Sam.

But the anger had gone now. Now all he had left were her photos, the letters and a mobile phone that her parents still hadn't cut off.

There was only one thing for it. He focused on making a perfect goats' cheese tortellini — Katherine's favourite.

6

By the time Lola had visited her father again, taken the bus with Babcia back to her house and settled her in, then walked back to the cafe, it was after seven o'clock. The kitchen light was on as Lola pushed open the back door. Sam was working at the bench, his hands tweaking and turning pasta.

'Hi,' she said, with a friendly but nervous smile. It was so awkward she could die. Like some sort of speed-dating experiment for flatmates. But then she thought of her dad and realised things could be worse. *Nut up and get on with it*, Lola, she told herself. *This is how it has to be for now.*

'Hi yourself,' he said, glancing up at her. 'How's your dad?'

'Same,' shrugged Lola. 'But the doctor seems to think it's

normal. The whole coma thing is freaking me out.'

Sam nodded, thinking of Katherine on life support. Her chest rising with each breath, giving everyone hope, but all the while the doctors saying she was brain dead.

Lola walked over and looked at his work. 'Little ears,' she said admiringly.

Sam glanced at her and smiled. He looked a little less hippie now that he'd changed, she noticed.

'Little ears indeed. I thought we could do an orecchiette with a nice ragù sauce. I know it's peasant-style food, but we can buy cheap cuts of meat and slow-cook the sauce. I also made goats' cheese tortellini. For tomorrow's lunch special.'

Lola nodded, impressed. 'Nothing wrong with peasant food. Remember I'm half-Polish, half-convict.' She heard her stomach rumble as she took her hair down from her bun.

'You eaten?' Sam asked her, raising an eyebrow at the sound of her stomach.

'Not since this morning,' she admitted.

'I'll make you something.'

Lola smiled. 'You don't need to do that. I can just have some toast.'

'Nope, I insist,' he replied. 'Never pick a fight with a cook, we'll always win.'

'Ain't that the truth,' laughed Lola.

He set to work, boiling water and taking a lemon, some white bread and a couple of cloves of garlic.

'Did you go upstairs?' she asked him.

'Yes, I assume I'm in the room with the cookbooks.'

'Yep,' said Lola, wondering if he had snooped in her room. She would have totally snooped if she were him, but then she was a girl. Didn't all girls snoop? 'So, you're travelling? Doing the backpacking thing?'

'Uh huh,' said Sam, putting a big pinch of salt into the boiling water. 'It's great,' he lied. 'I've met some great people, seen amazing things, you know.'

'What amazing things have you seen?'

Sam thought about the fact that he hadn't see anything, really. Besides the city, that beautiful pier, and of course the inside of the hostel. But could he say that to her? Probably not. 'I haven't been here long and, you know, money's tight. So I haven't seen as much as I'd like,' he said vaguely, as he dropped the pasta into the boiling water and started to make the breadcrumbs.

Lola nodded but felt confused. Why would he say he had seen amazing things and then not give any more information? She sat up on the bench and crossed her legs. 'Why do you like cooking?' she asked him.

Sam shrugged. 'I actually like tasting more than cooking. When something hits your tongue and everything in your brain changes. You know that feeling?'

'Yep, I'm like that with chocolate. I can have the worst thing happen, and then I'll eat chocolate and things will improve – at least in my head, anyway.'

'Have you eaten any today?' he asked as he stirred the pasta.

'No,' she exclaimed, stunned at the realisation. 'That's why things are so shitty!'

Sam pan-fried the garlic and breadcrumbs and then went back into the coolroom, returning with a container of white anchovies. 'Will you eat these?'

Lola looked. 'Oh god, yes.'

Sam added the delicate fish to the breadcrumbs and the garlic, threw in some parsley from the bunch in the jug of water on the bench, and squeezed a little lemon juice over the top. He then drained the pasta, tossed it into the frying pan and mixed it with the other ingredients over the flame before pouring it into two bowls.

Lola leant back and grabbed two forks from the dish rack behind her. She handed one to Sam.

She took her first mouthful. The first taste was of fresh anchovies, but then the lemon and garlic with little crispy bits of bread came to the fore. It was a perfect combination with the homemade pasta. So simple, but with subtle layers of flavour. 'Man, this is good,' she said as she ate greedily. She was suddenly starving.

Sam laughed as he watched her eat.

Lola didn't care what he thought of her eating habits. It had been almost twelve hours since she'd eaten, and she'd been to hell and back that day. She was hungry, and the food was amazing.

They ate in comfortable silence.

Putting down the bowl after she finished, Lola smiled at Sam. 'Bloody great,' she said.

Sam just smiled his thanks as he finished his food, but Lola could tell he was pleased with her review.

She jumped off the bench and went to the fridge at the back of the kitchen, pulling out the rest of the chocolate cake from the party the night before.

'Milk?' she asked, putting the cake on the bench and getting out a knife.

'Pardon?'

'Glass of milk? With your cake?'

Sam hadn't drunk a glass of milk since he was a kid. He looked quizzically at Lola.

'You have to have milk with chocolate cake,' she said seriously. 'They're perfect together.' She pushed a slice of cake towards him, then took out a carton of milk and took two glasses from the industrial dishwasher. She poured them both a glass and then handed him a fork.

'Go for it.'

She dug her fork into the cake. Sam took a small bite, and then another, and another.

'Now drink the milk,' ordered Lola as she took a sip. She felt the milk leaving a little beaded moustache on her lip.

Sam did as she said and then smiled at her. 'You're right. It's excellent.'

'Excellent,' said Lola, mimicking his accent. 'I like your accent.

You sound like Harry Potter.'

Sam threw his head back and laughed. 'And you look like a Weasley, with that hair,' he countered.

Lola laughed. They fell silent as they picked at the dessert.

'Thank you for helping,' said Lola sincerely, taking her empty plate and glass to the sink, rinsing them and then putting them in the·dishwasher. 'I'd be absolutely done for, if you weren't here.'

'Thanks for trusting me. I promise not to let you down.'

They looked at each other for a moment.

'All right, I'm going to bed,' Lola said, aware she was blushing slightly but not really sure why. 'I have so much to do tomorrow.' She looked up at the clock above Sam's head. Eight o'clock. Her flight to London would be leaving in two hours. She should have been at the airport, going through customs.

Lola climbed the stairs and headed into her bedroom, flopping down on her bed. *Everything happens for a reason*, Babcia had said on the bus ride home. But there was no good reason, as far as she could see, for something like this to happen to her dad.

No, the only thing that this proved was that the world was a mixed-up place, where a woman could leave her child in order to fulfill her own selfish dreams, shattering her husband's dreams along the way. And now that husband was lying in a coma because he didn't look both ways before carrying a box of basil across the road.

It's all so dramatic, she thought as she rolled over and punched her pillow. She got up and cleaned her teeth, went to the toilet and then went back to her room, locking the door and shifting her large armchair against it, just to be safe.

And then she slept.

~

Lola's alarm went off at six o'clock. She reached across to hit the snooze button before remembering that her life had changed. Completely. It wasn't a terrible dream; it was real. She pulled herself out of bed, moved the chair and unlocked the door.

The door to her father's room was open, and she could see the bed was neatly made. The only sign of Sam was his backpack in the corner. She could hear noises coming from downstairs in the kitchen.

After going to the bathroom, Lola tiptoed back down the hallway and slipped into her father's room. She crossed the floor and opened Sam's backpack. Some clothes, toiletries, a passport holder. She pulled out the passport and opened it.

'Samuel William Button,' she read. His surname made her laugh. *Sam Button*, she repeated in her head. *Gold*.

She went through his details and saw he was twenty-two. He only had one stamp in his passport, the Australian one. She was putting the passport back into the holder when she saw the edge of a photograph and pulled it out. It was Sam, with clean short hair, a big grin and his arms around a pretty brunette.

They look happy, she thought as she tucked the photo back

where she had found it. She wondered why the girlfriend wasn't travelling with him. Had they broken up? Was she coming to join him soon?

Back in her room, she rang the hospital. Her father was stable, and his breathing had regulated. But they were still keeping him in the coma. Lola missed him so much it hurt. It was too early to ring Babcia, so she dressed in jeans, a blue-and-white striped T-shirt and her pink Converse. At the last minute she tied a green scarf in her hair and, with a sigh, headed downstairs to the kitchen.

Kelsey was already sorting out plates and glasses, and Sam was moving about the space as though he had worked there all his life. He moved gracefully around the benches and stoves, like a dancer. The kitchen was clearly a second home to him.

'Morning,' he said cheerfully, looking up at her.

'Meh,' said Lola but with a smile.

'How's David?' asked Kelsey.

'Improving but still unconscious,' Lola said as she opened the back door and picked up the crate of milk that been delivered.

'I hope you don't mind, but I rewrote the menu on the chalk-board out the front,' said Sam. 'Just so people know what's what.'

'That's fine, thanks,' said Lola as she dragged the crate to the coolroom. She liked the way Sam just made the decisions that needed to be made. It meant there were fewer decisions for her tired brain to cope with.

Fiona was warming up the coffee machine, so Lola started to drag the tables outside and set up the white umbrellas. It was going to be a lovely sunny day. Before long, the first customers started arriving for their coffee.

By eight-thirty, Lola was run off her feet, Fiona was working up a sweat over the coffee machine and Kelsey had been racing between the tables and the kitchen all morning. The only person in his element was Sam, who was literally humming along as he worked. He was calm but super efficient.

Lola was impressed as each dish came out with something special added to it. The dollar pancakes, with the dusting of icing sugar and strawberry compote on the side, looked delicious. The eggs Benedict, with a garnish of cress instead of parsley, looked like something from a magazine. The boiled eggs with faces drawn on them were a hit with the children — as well as a few adults, who smiled broadly as they were put in front of them. *So simple, popular and playful*, thought Lola as she carried out another serve to a guy sitting at the communal table.

'People love those boiled eggs,' she said as she went back into the kitchen.

'Yeah, it reminds them of when they were kids,' said Sam easily.

Lola laughed. 'I always had *pączki* for breakfast when I was at my grandma's. Here, I would just grab a croissant.' She put a dirty plate into the sink and threw the eggshells in the bin.

'What did you have?'

'*Pączki*,' said Lola. 'Polish donuts. You ever had one?'

'Nope,' said Sam, as he mashed avocado and feta onto toast.

'I'll get Babcia to make you some one day.'

For a moment there, Lola realised she had forgotten to worry about her dad and how she was going to keep the cafe running. She grabbed a coffee and took it into the courtyard, sitting on an old milk crate. Her phone rang in her pocket.

'Hello?' she answered, seeing it was a private number.

'Viola Batko? This is Dr Peterson. From the Alfred Hospital.'

Lola froze. 'Yes?' she said, her voice barely audible.

She saw Sam walk out with a bag of rubbish and throw it into the bin. He frowned at her and made an enquiring face.

'We're going to bring your father out of his coma, now that the swelling is subsiding. Did you want to be here?'

Lola closed her eyes. 'I'll be right there.' She shoved the phone into her pocket and stood up. 'I have to go,' she said to Sam and, without another word, ran upstairs, grabbed her bag and left for the hospital.

7

'How is he?' asked Sam that evening as Lola, having slowly climbed the stairs, walked into the sitting room.

Sam was on the sofa, the reading lamp on behind him and a copy of *The Joy of Pasta* in his hands. Lola smiled at the book and then at Sam.

'You're a food dork,' she teased, feeling the lightness of knowing her father was at least conscious. 'He's okay,' she added, answering his question. 'Considering. Has a killer headache, and he didn't say much. You know, when they told me he was coming out of the coma I expected it to be like it is on TV. A dramatic waking up, lots of kissing and hugging. But it's not — he just kind of fluttered his eyes, said my name, and then passed out again.

It was actually kind of underwhelming, to be honest.' Lola realised she was rambling, and joking to lighten the mood. The truth was, hearing her dad say her name had made her sob like a little girl lost at the playground. She fell into the armchair opposite Sam.

'Well, he's alive and out of the coma,' he said simply.

Again, she noticed how calm Sam was. She wondered if he meditated or something. After all, he did seem like a hippie. Or a faux hippie, maybe.

His feet were bare and he was wearing shorts and a white T-shirt, but he'd obviously showered. He had damp hair and smelled fresh.

'What's been happening here?' she asked, suddenly aware of how dishevelled she must look.

'Kelsey took the takings to the bank and Fiona left you a note, which I put next to the mail,' Sam said, gesturing to the desk, which was piled high with papers and envelopes.

Dad may be an amazing chef and fabulous man, but he is clearly terrible at administration, thought Lola, grabbing the note and the mail.

'I'm stuffed,' she said. 'I'm gonna shower and go to bed.'

Sam nodded and caught her eye. 'Hey, I'm really glad your dad's okay.'

Lola felt tears well up and blinked to make them disappear. 'Thanks, so am I.' In her room, she opened the note from Fiona first, which she had sealed in an envelope.

Hi,

I asked around about Sam at the hostel. Nothing bad to report. Nice guy apparently, quiet — didn't make any friends but didn't make any enemies either.

He was great in the cafe today, even served and helped clear tables when we were run off our feet. I don't think you should worry, but sleep with the door locked just in case.

Fi

Lola put down the note and opened the mail. One bill after another. *So many bills*, she thought, *so little money*. She left them next to her bed. *Tomorrow*, she promised herself. *I'll sort them all out tomorrow*.

Seeing her father that afternoon, she realised how close he came to being brain damaged, or dying. She could have been an orphan.

What she hadn't told Sam was that her dad had been really confused and upset. He'd fall asleep and then wake up, asking the same questions each time. He kept asking when she'd got back from London. She'd had to keep explaining she hadn't gone yet, which made her dad cry each time. The doctor had said it was normal, but it scared Lola.

Babcia had tried her best to calm him too. 'Stop vorrying, David,' she'd said, gently stroking his hair. 'It vill be all right, Lola is smart. She vill handle everything.'

Babcia's faith in her was heartening, but Lola didn't understand why her dad was so emotional or why he'd think she'd been to London already.

'It's the swelling in the brain, it's bruised,' Dr Peterson had said. 'Just be patient. Hopefully we'll see a little improvement each day.'

Lola was too tired to shower, and just lay on the bed. She was still wondering if she should push her dresser against the door when she drifted off to sleep.

When the alarm woke her the next morning she realised she had slept in her clothes, but at some point during the night had climbed under the covers. The sound of the shower across the hall reminded her she wasn't alone. She lay in bed, thinking.

She needed to get some routine happening. Lola had always hated routine; she'd always found it insulting for society to tell her what to do and when to do it. But now she realised she would have to get on with it and put her high and mighty views aside, at least while she was running the cafe.

As she got out of bed, she stood on the pile of bills from the night before. She made a face at them as she grabbed her pink fluffy robe and padded to the bathroom, which was now empty. As she showered she was thankful for the lock on the door. When she was done she made a mad dash for her bedroom, even though there was no sign of Sam.

Lola looked at her clothes and then pulled some stuff from her backpack. A black ruffled miniskirt and a white tank top would be her look for the day, with her comfy yellow jelly sandals. Applying red lip gloss, she tied her wet hair into a bun at the nape of her neck and at the last minute put in some oversized fake pearl earrings.

She looked at herself in the mirror. She looked okay. Maybe even responsible enough to run a cafe and go through all those bills. She gathered the paperwork from the floor and grabbed the ledger and portable file from her dad's desk.

Downstairs she could hear Sam moving about in the kitchen and the sounds of the coffee machine warming up, the familiar clatter of cutlery and crockery.

Lola stood at the top of the stairs and suddenly thought about her mother. *What is she doing now?* she wondered. Then she heard the smash of what sounded like a glass or six, and Fiona swearing.

Lola went downstairs and into the kitchen. She nodded at Sam, who nodded back. 'You okay?' she asked Fiona as she put her head through the servery window.

'Yeah, fine,' said Fiona grumpily.

Lola caught Kelsey's eye. She shook her head at Lola and mimed drinking with her hand.

'Hangover, huh?' asked Lola with a smile.

Fiona moaned. 'You have no idea.'

Lola laughed as she walked out into the cafe, dumped the paperwork on a table near the kitchen door, and returned to the kitchen.

'How are you, Sam?' she asked, watching him as he expertly julienned red capsicums.

'Good thanks. And you, Lola?'

They were so polite it was painful.

He was breaking eggs into a big silver bowl now, and Lola was transfixed as his hands moved. It was a beautiful thing to watch.

'You said you're not a trained chef,' she said, frowning.

'I'm not.'

'You work like a chef.'

'I taught myself from YouTube,' he said, turning his back to her.

Before Lola could say anything, she heard the ring of the cafe door as the first customer arrived. Sam pushed a basket of pastries towards her.

'Take these out, will you?'

Lola looked down at the perfect croissants and pains au chocolat. 'Sam, you're amazing.'

'It's nothing,' he said casually.

'Nothing but amazing,' she replied, and watched him blush. He was cute, she realised. In his hippie, food-dorky way.

She walked out into the cafe, gratefully accepted a coffee from Fiona and, taking a pen from the counter, went to the table where her pile of responsibility sat waiting.

Lola had never been the most organised girl, either at school or at home, and now, as she sat with the papers, file and ledger, she wondered what on earth she should do with them all. She opened the file and saw her father had a basic filing system for bills – if you could call shoving them in alphabetically, some still unopened, a system. Every one of them had several follow-up letters, and the water bill now had a disconnection letter stapled to it.

Lola went through the bills from last night. There was a final letter; the water would be cut off at five that afternoon unless she paid the three hundred and seventy-two dollars.

She wrote down the due dates for the utilities, and then the amounts. *Total $1258.90*, she wrote carefully on a spare ordering pad.

And that didn't include the suppliers. She went to get another coffee. The cafe was filling up now, with commuters waiting for takeaways and a few people having breakfast in.

'I thought you were heading off to London,' Lola heard a surprised voice say, as she took her coffee from Kelsey and went back to her seat. Lola looked up and saw an appliquéd koala wearing a cork hat. Little sequined 'corks' dangled from the strings on the hat, giving the jumper a 3D quality that Lola found both creepy and hilarious.

'Oh, hey,' said Lola, smiling up at the woman, formerly of the ice-skating bear jumper. 'No, my dad's had an accident. So I'm staying to help out.'

The woman looked concerned. 'That's terrible. Is he okay?'

'He will be,' said Lola, 'but it was pretty bad. He's going to be in rehab for a while, so I'll be taking care of things until he's better.'

'Poor David. And what a shame to have to put off your trip. But you're a good daughter for helping out.'

'I didn't really have a choice,' said Lola, before realising how bitter that sounded. 'I mean, of course I'd stay and help. I wouldn't just leave him.'

'Of course,' said the woman kindly.

She has such a pretty face, Lola thought, *but her choice in jumpers is criminal*. The woman must have been about forty, and was wearing nondescript jeans and runners, no jewellery and a little bit of makeup: mascara and frosted lipstick that was completely outdated. In fact, everything about this woman was outdated. It was almost back in fashion, it was so old school.

'I'm Lola,' she said.

'Jane,' the woman smiled. She looked at the pile of paperwork on the table. 'So, you're taking over the books, too?'

'Trying to,' sighed Lola. 'But it's proving to be hideous.' She gave a hollow laugh.

Jane looked at Lola with a shy smile. 'Maybe I can help you. I'm a bookkeeper, you know.'

Lola shook her head. 'I don't know what that is, but if you can tell me what to do to make sense of this mess, then awesome. Please sit down.'

Jane sat down on the chair opposite Lola.

'Would you like a latte, Jane?' said Lola.

'Yes please,' said Jane as Lola handed her the file, the ledger and the pile of new bills.

Lola went and made Jane's coffee, while Kelsey was making three chai teas.

'Who's your friend?' she asked Lola.

'Jane. A customer. She's a bookkeeper,' said Lola. 'Although I have no idea what that is.'

'They go through your accounts and do your tax and stuff,' explained Kelsey. 'My sister's one back home.'

Lola put the coffee down in front of Jane, who looked up from the ledger.

'How's it look?' asked Lola.

'Does your dad have any accounting software?' asked Jane.

Lola shook her head. 'Dad doesn't really get computers,' she said, recalling how he made a face at her whenever she suggested he use her laptop for anything.

Jane shrugged. 'I don't get that. I love them.'

Lola nodded in agreement. So, Jane liked computers, but dressed as though she was living in the eighties. *What's with this woman?* wondered Lola.

'So what's the story?' asked Lola. 'What do I need to do?'

Jane paused. 'I really need to see everything, including bank statements, so I can put it all together and work that out.'

Lola grimaced. 'How much would that cost?' *Maybe Jane could sleep in the living room and do it for a cheaper price*, she thought dryly. Maybe that was the answer to all her problems: everyone could have room and board and they would work for nothing . . .

'How about I just help you understand your position? It won't take more than a few hours, and you can give me a week of free coffees in return,' suggested Jane.

Lola laughed. 'That doesn't seem fair to you.'

'It's fine, honestly. I can see you need help, and this is what I do. And I love coffee.'

Lola reached out and impulsively hugged the woman and her corked koala jumper. 'You're ace, Jane. Thank you so, so much.'

For the second time in forty-eight hours, Lola felt that things might just be okay.

8

Lola had arranged for Babcia to be taken to the hospital by taxi every second afternoon. Lola would visit at night, and David's friends would stop by the hospital whenever they could.

Lola handed all the paperwork over to Jane, including the bank statements and invoices and all the other bits of paper she could find lying around her dad's desk. Jane had said she'd come back to Lola with a plan by lunchtime that day.

Lola was sitting in the kitchen, drinking coffee and eating a croissant as she watched Sam work at the kitchen bench.

'You are so a chef,' she laughed, as he expertly boned a chicken.

Sam looked up at her and made a guilty face. 'Okay, I can't fool you,' he admitted. 'But I only worked for a few months after finishing culinary school in London. I need loads more experience.'

'Why did you leave then?' she asked him, wondering if she should go and get another croissant. They were amazing.

Sam was silent as he cut the chicken into pieces. 'Things changed,' he said eventually. 'Life throws surprises at you. You know how it is.'

Lola nodded. 'I sure do. I'm supposed to be where you came from, and instead I'm here, trying to run a business.' She shook her head as her phone chimed with a text message from Rosie.

How's your dad? Have you seen the new cafe up the road from you? Got a review in the paper today. Rx

Lola stood up and rushed into the cafe, grabbing the paper from the communal table and flipping to the food section. Her eyes scanned quickly as she took in the review. She walked back into the kitchen, holding the paper.

'What's up?' asked Sam easily as he came out the coolroom.

'There's a new cafe up the road,' she said. 'Where the florist's used to be. I didn't even know it had opened.'

Sam shrugged. 'It doesn't matter. There are enough caffeine addicts to go round.'

Lola cleared her throat before she read aloud from the review. 'Blueberry Cafe is the type of establishment this street has been begging for. Fashionable, with a friendly vibe, the food is restaurant quality without the old-school style that this strip has become known for.' She raised her eyes to Sam angrily. 'They mean us.'

Sam frowned. 'That's a bit harsh.'

Lola leant back against the bench and threw the paper down. 'Shit.' They stood in silence for a few moments.

'What do you think of the cafe?' Lola asked suddenly.

'What do you mean?'

Lola shrugged. 'I'm asking your opinion. I want to know what you think of the cafe – the food, the atmosphere, the staff. You tell me, I've lived here all my life, I have no idea.'

Sam paused, and Lola realised he had thought about it before. He was obviously weighing up how to tell her what he thought.

'Come on, don't be soft about it,' she assured him. 'I can handle anything.'

'Soft? Jesus, you're tough,' he laughed.

Lola crossed her arms and waited.

Sam put his head through the servery window and spoke to Kelsey, who quickly handed him an espresso and a latte.

'Come on,' he said to Lola, who followed him to the back door.

The sunlight poured into the courtyard and it was warm and pleasant. Wild jasmine ran along the fence, and the scent was delicious. Lola sat on a milk crate next to Sam and watched as he stirred his espresso.

'Hit me,' she said, waiting for Sam's review.

He spoke slowly. 'I think Cafe Ambrosia is great. Warm and old-school. But to really compete, it needs something new. Something for people in the area to get excited about.'

Lola nodded. Hearing Sam say that made her realise it was

true. But her dad hated change. Nothing had really changed since her mother had walked out the door.

She sipped her coffee. 'What would you do if the cafe were yours?'

Sam laughed. 'Oh god, what wouldn't I do?

'I want details. Tell me what you would do.'

The sun was warming her bones, and Sam was warming to the idea.

Just as he was about to speak, Fiona popped her head out. 'I need an eggs Benedict, Sam. And Lol? There's a woman in a horrendous top to see you.'

Lola stood up and took her coffee into the kitchen. She dumped it in the sink before heading out into the cafe.

Jane was standing by the counter. In her hands were the file and the ledger.

'That was quick,' said Lola with a smile. 'I thought you were coming in at lunchtime.'

Jane shook her head and gestured to the table where they had sat the day before. Lola felt a knot of dread tighten in her stomach, just like it used to before a maths test.

'How bad is it?' she asked Jane, looking at the sparkly-horned unicorn adorning her T-shirt.

Jane opened the ledger, pulled out a piece of paper and put it in front of Lola.

'This is how much you owe,' she explained, pointing to one column, 'this is how much the cafe is earning each week. This is the money in the bank, and this is the average cost the cafe takes to run every week.'

Lola looked at the columns. She didn't have to be a mathematician to understand there was an imbalance. She swallowed and felt herself having some sort of a hot flush. Maybe she was having her first panic attack?

'Why didn't Dad say anything?' she said, thinking of the money he had given her for her plane ticket, and the extra money he had put into her account to cover her until she got a job in London. She thought of the money he had spent on her going-away party, and how she hadn't really helped him with anything. She had just taken from him. Lola felt a lump rising in her throat.

'Maybe he doesn't realise how close it is to the line,' said Jane, leaning forward. 'Many creative types aren't really across their finances.'

Lola shook her head. 'What can I do? There's a new cafe up the road that might take our customers. If it's this tough now, it's only going to get worse with competition.'

She felt like crying, but refused to tear up in front of everyone. She had to hold herself together.

Jane looked around at the half-full cafe. 'You need to increase the money coming in and control the money going out. It's simple in theory but hard to do in real life, I know.'

'Thanks, Jane,' Lola said with a rueful smile.

'I'm sorry to be the bearer of bad news.'

Lola shook her head. 'It's fine. It'll work out.' She thought that maybe, if she said it often enough, it might become true.

Jane looked at her notes. 'Also, your dad needs to do his tax. He's had several reminder notices already.'

'I don't know anything about that stuff,' frowned Lola.

'Does he have a box of receipts or a file or something? Anything besides this one?' She patted the file in front of her.

Lola thought. 'Yeah, he has one upstairs. I didn't think to give it to you.'

'That's fine, I can go through it all and file your tax returns, if you want to go through the receipts with me.'

'I'd be useless at that. We might need to wait till Dad comes out of hospital.'

'You don't have time, Lola. David's risking a serious fine if he doesn't comply.'

'Could you go and see him?' Lola asked suddenly. 'In hospital?' Her dad's confusion seemed to have lifted, so she figured it was worth a try. 'I'll call him before, to explain you're coming.'

'Are you sure he's up to it?' asked Jane, and Lola could have sworn she was blushing.

'I hope so,' said Lola. 'We don't have a choice anyway.'

Jane handed her a few bills with Post-it notes annotating them. 'These need to be paid now. I rang the water company and got you an extension. Special circumstances.'

'Shit, I forgot about the water bill,' said Lola, closing her eyes for a moment. 'There's so much to think about.'

'You'll be okay. You seem like a smart, sensible girl.'

Lola thought she was the least sensible girl she knew. 'There's just one thing,' she said hesitantly.

'Yes?'

'You know when I first met you, I said I was going to see my mother?'

Jane nodded.

'Dad doesn't know that's what I was planning. She broke his heart when she left him. I was just a baby. Having to look after me all these years has kind of . . . held him back. Even though he would never say it. So I don't want him to know I was going to find her, because then he'd think perhaps he hadn't given me enough or whatever. And then it all gets a bit Jerry Springer, you know? Does any of this make sense?'

Jane smiled. 'Of course. I doubt we'll talk about anything personal, but if we do, then I would never betray your confidence.' She stood up. 'I have to go to my next client now, but I've left my mobile number on the front of the bills, so call anytime. I'll come by after I've seen your father, and we can work out a system.'

Lola grimaced. 'I'm not so great with routine and order,' she confessed.

'You'll be fine, I promise,' said Jane as she left with a wave.

Lola took the paperwork and walked into the kitchen.

'You busy tonight?' she asked Sam.

'Nope, why?'

'I need you.'

'Always nice to be needed,' said Sam.

He looked up, and Lola thought maybe he was blushing. Or was she imagining it? 'We need to brainstorm the reinvention of Cafe Ambrosia.'

'Excellent,' he said. 'I love a good brainstorm.'

'I'm going to see Dad now. Talk later?'

'Sure thing,' said Sam as Lola walked towards the stairs. 'Oh, I forgot to say, I made some soup for your dad.'

Lola blinked a few times. 'Really?' She was surprised, and touched.

'I figured if hospitals here are anything like they are in the UK, then the food will be rubbish.'

Lola briefly wondered whether Sam had ever been in hospital, but then she glanced at the clock and realised she didn't have time to ask. She filed it away in her brain to bring up later.

'Sam?'

He looked up at her.

'Thanks.'

And she ran up the stairs before he could say anything in reply.

9

Lola arrived at the hospital a little while later, holding the care package from Sam.

In it was a thermos of minestrone soup, some crusty bread for dipping, and a little package of sea salt, pepper, freshly cut parsley and parmesan cheese. Lola had snatched one of her espresso-iced chocolate cupcakes from the counter and added it to the bounty as she left for the hospital.

Lola watched her dad from the doorway of his room. He was in bed, his head turned to the window. He looked frail and old and Lola felt a tug at her heart.

'Hi, Dad,' she said with forced cheer.

He turned at the sound of her voice. 'Lollipop. I was just thinking about you.' He smiled at her.

Lola put the bag on the table next to him and took out the thermos of soup, opening it and pouring it into the bowl that Sam had packed. She set up the seasoning and cheese next to it and laid out a napkin, putting the bread on it.

'Wow, look at this,' David said, as Lola leant over and inhaled the scent of the steaming Italian soup. 'Have you been cooking something other than cupcakes?'

Lola smiled. 'No way, but our new chef has.'

'New chef? I was going to ask if you'd called a temp agency to get someone to cover for me.' He tasted the soup and then sprinkled the cheese and parsley. 'It's perfectly seasoned,' he said, taking a noisy slurp. 'Who is this chef and how much are you paying him?'

'His name is Sam, he's a backpacker, and he is being paid what he deserves,' she said, not wanting to get into the sticky details about Sam sleeping in her dad's bed.

David tore off some bread and dipped it in the soup. 'You have no idea how good this is,' he said. 'There was a chicken dish at lunch that looked like it had drowned itself from shame in the pond of gravy it was floating in. I didn't touch it.'

Lola smiled and watched with pleasure as he ate hungrily. 'How are you feeling?'

'Marvellous,' he said, wiping the soup dripping down his chin with the napkin.

'Really?' asked Lola with a shake of her head. 'You know, you don't have to pretend. You have a broken pelvis and a head injury.'

'No really, I'm bloody great,' he said. 'I'm alive, and that's a great start to life.' He chuckled to himself as he wiped the bread around the now-empty bowl and chewed it with his eyes closed.

'Um, Dad?' In her head Lola had decided she'd go and speak to the doctor before she left the hospital. She remembered from one of those medical shows that people sometimes had changes in their personality after head injuries. He'd never been like this. She wondered if they were monitoring him properly.

David looked at Lola closely. 'I don't want to keep living like I was,' he said, his eyes filling with tears.

Lola swallowed. What the heck was going on?

'I waited all those years for your mum to come back. And of course, she never did. When I was hit by that car, all I remember thinking is, *This is it. And I've wasted my life.* You know, the only thing I have to show for myself is you, and now you're all grown up and ready to live your own life. I need to sort myself out.'

He father never spoke like this; he was always quiet, thoughtful. He was kind, of course, but he showed very little emotion. She used to think he was a bit too boring and dependable. Now he had a faraway gleam in his eye she'd never seen before.

'I plan on living each moment to the fullest,' he said, brandishing the napkin like it was a flag of victory or something. 'As soon as I get out of here.'

'Okay,' said Lola, still unsure whether all this was because of the head injury, or a fabulous new lease of life after a near-death experience. One thing was for sure: she wasn't going to give him the espresso-laced cupcake. God knew he didn't need a sugar and caffeine hit, with his emotions all over the place like this.

Lola walked around the bed, packing up the crockery and brushing away the crumbs.

'Hand it over,' he said.

What?' asked Lola, looking in the bag and pretending there was nothing else.

'The cake. I can smell chocolate.' He shot Lola a look that she knew. 'Don't ever keep me away from chocolate.'

'I think you've gone mad,' she said, pulling out the cupcake container and putting it on the table.

He reached out and took her hands in his, holding them tight.

'No, Lola, don't you see? I was mad before. Now I feel myself again. This accident knocked some sense into me. I am going to change my life, from top to bottom. I'm going to do everything I've stopped myself doing these past eighteen years.'

Lola felt a flutter of fear in her stomach. It was one thing for her to think these things, but it was another to hear her dad saying them. 'What sort of things?'

He dropped her hands and reached over to open the container. He sniffed her cupcake and beamed at her.

'I don't know yet. But that's the best part, not knowing. But I tell you, I am ready for anything. To travel the world, cook amazing food, fall in love.'

Before Lola could speak she heard a knock on the door and there was Jane, in a different outfit from that morning. Now she was wearing a peacock T-shirt. It wasn't quite as gaudy as her other tops. In fact, Lola nearly liked it. She noticed Jane was also wearing peacock feather earrings and had done her hair.

'Hi,' said Lola, both relieved and disappointed at the interruption. 'Dad, this is Jane. She's helping me with the books for the cafe, since I know jack-shit about maths. But I need you to help her sort out your tax returns. You should have done them every year, you know.' She realised she sounded like a nagging old woman.

David took the last bite of his cupcake and put out a hand for Jane to shake. He smiled broadly at her.

Lola tried to imagine how her dad looked to Jane. Clearly insane with the joy of not dying, a few days of stubble on his face and mouth full of cupcake.

Lola picked up her bags and walked to the door. 'Have fun,' she joked as she got to the doorway.

Turning around, she saw that they were staring into each other's eyes and hadn't even noticed she was leaving.

10

The cafe was proving to be a fantastic distraction, Sam realised as he went upstairs after work that evening. He took a quick shower and reflected on the fact that he hadn't felt sorry for himself once since he'd arrived at the cafe; he'd hardly had time to think about all that he'd lost.

He looked at himself in the steamed-up mirror. He was thin. He needed to eat more, but mostly he didn't feel like it. *Working with food will do that. So will having a broken heart.*

Wrapping his towel around his waist, he opened the bathroom door at the same time Lola opened her bedroom door. He'd assumed she was locked away in her room doing paperwork; the desk in the living room had been ransacked. Now that the door to her room was open he could see papers all over the floor. She looked stressed.

'Hi,' she said, a little too brightly.

He knew that voice. It was that 'I'm okay, don't ask me about anything, let's keep this all pretendy and light' voice.

'Hi,' he said, conscious he was half-nude. He walked towards his room. 'You still keen to brainstorm?'

Lola sighed, and he thought she looked tired.

'We don't have to,' he said, in his matching 'pretendy and light' voice.

He had actually been looking forward to talking about the cafe, though. He liked Lola's company, and brainstorming menu ideas meant he didn't have to talk about himself.

'No, we do have to,' said Lola, making a face. 'Have you eaten?'

He felt her eyes flickering over his thin torso. 'No, not yet.'

'I'll sort something out and meet you in the living room.'

'Shouldn't I do that? I'm the cook.'

'No, you've been cooking all day,' Lola said. 'Anyway, I feel like Indian.'

'I could make a curry.'

'Nah, I want the works. Naan bread, pakora, samosas.'

Sam laughed. 'Okay, I give in. I can't whip that up in half an hour.' He went into his room and dressed in jeans and a clean T-shirt. He ran his hands through his hair, trying to tame the bits that stuck up. He should get a haircut. When he walked out to the living room, Lola was in the corner of the sofa, a large pad of paper on her lap. She was holding a pink pen with a disco ball on the end of it. She gestured to the beers on the coffee table. 'I've ordered us a feast fit for a maharajah.'

'I should have made something.'

Lola turned her nose up. 'You sound like Dad.'

'Did he like the soup?' Sam asked, taking a sip of his beer.

'He loved the soup,' said Lola with a small smile. She paused.

'You okay?' he asked. She looked worried and upset.

'It's just . . . ' she trailed off, obviously looking for the right words. 'He just seems really different since the accident.'

'Different how?'

'He seems . . . ' she looked at Sam and shrugged. 'Crazy? I don't know. He's gone all YOLO on me.'

Sam burst out laughing. 'What's wrong with that?' he asked, thinking of his mum, up at five-thirty every morning, perky as anything about the day.

'But Dad's just not like that,' insisted Lola. 'I love him, but he's the most boring guy in the world.'

'Maybe he's tired of being boring.'

Sam put one foot on the coffee table and then remembered it wasn't his home and put it down.

'You can put it there,' said Lola. 'I don't mind.'

Sam resumed his position. 'I don't know your dad. I guess I don't really know you very well. But you want to go overseas as soon as your dad's better. So what does it matter how he lives his life when you're not around to see it?'

Lola frowned, and Sam thought she looked cute when she was pissed off.

'I guess. I mean, I wanted him to get his own life back. That was one of the reasons I wanted to go overseas. But still, he was weird. Trust me.' Lola waved the pen at him, clearly wanting to change the topic. 'You ready to start?'

'Yep. First, get free wi-fi. That's a no-brainer. I can get it installed tomorrow, if you want?'

Lola nodded. 'Yeah, that'd be great! I've been after Dad for ages about that.'

Encouraged, Sam continued. 'So, food goes in trends, as you know. Your dad's menu is totally fine, but it isn't exciting. People want to be delighted when the meal arrives. They want something they wouldn't think to make for themselves. Even if it's comfort food reinvented.'

Lola nodded. 'That's why your boiled eggs are so popular.'

Sam went through some breakfast and lunch ideas he'd been playing around with, and Lola wrote furiously. Every time she pressed down on the paper with the pen, the little silver disco ball lit up, highlighting her face. He found himself watching as she jotted down his suggestions.

'Make the food interesting,' she said as she wrote. She looked up at Sam. 'Unique.'

He nodded. 'Dinner?' he suggested, even though he hadn't really thought that through.

'Dinner?'

'Why not?' he asked, warming to the idea. He realised he kind of missed the bustle of the kitchen during dinner service. It had a different feel to working days. 'We wouldn't have to do it every night, maybe just two nights a week. A small, seasonal menu. It could be nice, and it brings in a lot more money than breakfasts and lunches.'

Lola tapped the disco ball on the paper. 'But you'd need a sous-chef, wouldn't you? We couldn't afford anyone else, or we'd lose any extra margin.'

'You could do it,' he said. 'You know how to cook, don't you?'

'I bake,' said Lola firmly.

'Bake, cook, whatever. You know your way around the kitchen.'

'We don't have a liquor licence.'

'Make it BYO. Everyone prefers that anyway. If it works, you can apply for a liquor licence later on.' Sam watched Lola's face as she sat in thought. 'Obviously our costs would go up initially,' he went on. 'We'd need more supplies.'

Lola looked at him as though he was crazy. 'I can't see how I can afford for our costs to go up.'

Sam paused. 'You could cash in your ticket. You'll be covered by your travel insurance, because of what happened. That could go towards it.'

'And I have my savings, and the money Dad and Babcia gave me,' Lola acknowledged.

'What were you going to do in London?' Sam asked, suddenly curious.

She was tapping the disco ball pen on her forehead. 'Huh?'

'What were you going to do over in London?'

Lola squinted at him for a moment, as though deciding whether he passed some sort of test. 'You know, just travel, meet people, hang out,' she said vaguely.

Clearly he had failed her test, whatever it was. For some reason that he couldn't quite understand, he was disappointed she hadn't confided in him.

The doorbell rang. 'That's our dinner,' she said, jumping up and heading downstairs.

A few minutes later she was back, the delicious smell of curry coming from a bag in one hand, two plates and forks in the other.

'I hope you like curry,' she said.

'Of course, it's like our national food in the UK.' Sam pulled his wallet out of his back pocket. 'What do I owe you?'

'Nothing. It's Sanjay's brother's restaurant. We get it for free half the time,' Lola said, opening a container of steaming saffron rice.

'That's very decent of him,' he said, thinking of the curry shop down the road from his place in London. No freebies there, apart from the occasional extra piece of naan.

Lola served them both, handing Sam a plate piled high with food before tucking into her own. She started to eat the butter chicken and rice, mopping it up with the bread and sipping her beer in between bites.

Sam laughed. 'You eaten today?' There was a little bit of yellow rice in her hair.

'Not since breakfast.'

Sam smiled.

'What?' She wiped her mouth self-consciously.

'You eat like you're starving.'

'So?' she countered with a shrug. 'I eat how I eat.'

'It wasn't a criticism,' he said. 'I like how you throw yourself into things. Like the cafe, the paperwork, your curry.'

Lola nodded. 'Yeah, I tend to do that. Life is not meant to be approached carefully, in my opinion. Just go for it.'

'Maybe your Dad has caught your disease.'

She shrugged. 'Maybe.'

She handed him a vegie samosa, and took one for herself. They ate in silence.

'Where's your mum, if you don't mind me asking?' Sam asked. He'd wondered that a few times in the last few days, but hadn't got around to asking.

'I don't know,' said Lola. 'She left when I was a baby.'

'Oh,' Sam said softly. He shouldn't have pried. 'That's a bit shite.'

'Oh, I don't care, I've got a great life,' said Lola as she scooped naan with curry into her mouth. Sam wondered if he detected a bit of the 'light and pretendy' in her voice.

'I meant for your mum,' said Sam. He found himself thinking of Katherine's mum. Everyone was devastated when Katherine died. But nothing was quite so heartbreaking as seeing her mum so forlorn. Sitting for hours in Katherine's room, refusing to eat. Her only child, gone in an instant. Sam didn't think she'd ever get over it.

Lola scowled. 'She left me, remember? She could have come back at any time.'

'Maybe, but who knows what was going on. She obviously had issues.'

'Obviously,' said Lola shortly.

They sat in silence.

'Is that why you were going overseas? To find her?'

Lola paused and then nodded slowly. 'Yeah. I was so excited and nervous, and I had all these reunion speeches planned in my head. And now none of them matter, and you know what?'

Sam shook his head. 'What?'

'I'm actually kind of relieved to have a reason not to go for a while. I want to go but I'm scared at the same time. Pathetic, huh?'

'Not at all. You need to find out why she left. But you might not like the reason.'

'I've always felt like I can't start my life until I know why she didn't want to be with me. Why she didn't want to be my mother.'

'Maybe she couldn't,' said Sam. 'Maybe she had stuff going on and she needed to sort her head out.'

Lola shrugged and licked her fingers. 'But no word in eighteen years? That's a pretty crap effort.'

Sam couldn't argue with that. But he knew that things were never that simple. People made choices that were hard to undo later in life.

'If you were stuck on a desert island and could only have four different ingredients for the rest of your life, what would they be?'

she asked suddenly, eating the last crunchy corner of her samosa and looking intently at him.

This girl was clearly into her food. He liked that about her. He pretended to think about her question, even though he often played this game with his family, and on long bus trips or whatever, and already knew his answer. 'Chicken, potatoes, garlic and cheese.' He counted them off on his fingers.

'Sensible Samuel Button!' Lola teased.

Sam wondered if she was flirting with him. 'Did I tell you my last name?' he asked, trying to remember.

'I saw it on your bank details.'

Sam laughed. 'Sensible, huh? Unlike you, kid. I bet you'd just take four different types of chocolate.'

Lola poked her tongue out at him. She stood up and packed up the plates and containers. 'All right, I'm gonna go to bed and do some planning for the cafe. Thanks for the company and the ideas.'

She walked downstairs to dump the rubbish and dishes. Sam sat in the chair, waiting for her return. *Was* she flirting with him? He had no idea. It had been so long since he'd had an actual conversation with a girl who didn't feel sorry for him, he'd forgotten all the rules.

Lola returned and picked up the pad and pen from the sofa. "Night, Sam,' she said, and walked into her room.

"Night,' said Sam softly.

No, she wasn't flirting, Sam told himself. She was just like that — bubbly, fun, confident. Gosh, confidence was sexy.

That night, for the first time since Katherine had died, he found himself thinking about a different girl.

11

Lola thumped downstairs. She was so tired, she wasn't sure if she was even properly awake. *I must still be dreaming*, she thought, because she was hearing Babcia's voice.

'No, that's not how you do it,' Babcia's voice was saying. 'Don't over-vork the dough.'

Lola stood still outside the kitchen door, blinking furiously, trying to wake up. *Oh god, it isn't a dream.* Babcia was in the kitchen. With Sam. Making something.

This realisation slapped her awake as she walked in and took in the sight of Babcia at the kitchen bench, a white chef's apron around her waist, her hands in a large silver mixing bowl.

'Um, hi?' said Lola, as Kelsey walked past her and put a latte into her hand.

'Hiya,' Sam said, as Babcia spooned jam into a glass jug. 'Babcia is showing me how to make *pączki*,' he explained, turning back to Babcia.

'You never showed *me* how to make them,' sniped Lola as she took a sip of her coffee.

'Because you say you don't like to make Polish things.' Babcia gave an exaggerated eye-roll. 'I cannot teach you if you don't like.'

'Babcia,' said Lola, the coffee finally taking effect. 'Why are you here? And how do you know Sam?'

'I came to help. And so I met Sam. He says you gave him job, he is a nice boy.' Babcia affectionately touched Sam on the arm, leaving a smudge of flour there as a sort of mark of approval.

Sam looked at Lola pointedly. 'I explained to her that I live at the hostel and I come in very early,' he said. Lola nodded, grateful that he'd known not to say anything about living upstairs. Babcia and her old-fashioned values were kind of a package.

'You don't need to help, Babcia,' said Lola as she started to dry the cutlery from the dishwasher.

Babcia's face fell. 'But I like to help.'

Lola took the cutlery into the cafe and then started to refill the sugar bowls.

'Your grandmother is nice,' said Sam from behind her, making Lola jump.

'She's okay. She can be annoying.'

'She's bored, she needs a purpose. Let her find one here,' Sam said gently.

'You say that now, but she'll annoy you too,' said Lola with a small laugh.

'Maybe, maybe not,' said Sam. 'People tend to get more annoyed by their own families. Mine drive me mad. But as Mum says, they're all I have and I should be patient, in case they're not there one day. Go easy on her.'

Lola turned and looked at him, one hand on her hip. 'Don't tell me about family not being there. If you want to babysit my babcia, then fine. But don't give me a guilt trip.' She slammed a bowl down on the table, small crystals of sugar spilling everywhere.

'Lola, I —' Sam started, but Lola had already walked out the front door.

She walked up the street to cool off. The sun wasn't high yet, but she knew it was going to be a scorcher of a day.

Bloody Sam, she thought as she walked past the new cafe. She didn't know why it annoyed her so much to see Babcia and Sam bonding over dough. But it did. Babcia was always acting like she was the boss of everyone and now she was flirting with Sam, acting all pathetic around him. Lola knew it was childish to storm off like that, but she'd been so angry she couldn't help it.

She peered through the window at Blueberry Cafe, recognising a few faces from Cafe Ambrosia.

There's obviously no loyalty in the world of coffee, she thought dryly.

She had walked a little further before she realised she hadn't crossed the road to avoid the second-hand store. For the first time in her memory, she was standing right there, looking through the window of the forbidden shop. Arranged in the window was an ancient pair of wooden snowshoes next to a large taxidermy turtle and a Union Jack flag. Weird.

Lola put her hands to the glass to block out the glare and get a closer look. As soon as her eyes adjusted, she saw the old man was in the shop – and he was staring back at her.

She jumped back in fright before peering in again. This time the man waved. Tentatively she raised her hand in reply. Half to be polite and half to annoy Babcia, who was up to her elbows in *pączki* with Sam.

A moment later she heard the sound of the door unlocking.

'Lola?' she heard as the man stepped out of the dark shop.

She didn't know what she had been expecting, but she certainly hadn't thought the man would know her name, let alone say it in such a gentle, friendly way.

He was in grey pants and a shirt and tie. His clothes looked scrupulously clean, but had seen better days. He looked as old as Babcia.

'Um, hi,' she said, all the suspicions about him over the years crowding her brain. 'How do you know my name?

He smiled at her sadly. 'I knew your mother,' he said gently. He looked over her shoulder, as though he was waiting for someone to come and tell him off for talking to her.

Lola stood very still. 'Then why don't I know you?'

'I'm Clyde Cheevers.' He put out his hand and Lola shook

it. The papery skin of his hand was cool. He gestured for Lola to come inside the shop. 'I think it's time we got to know each other.'

Lola paused. Her instincts told her Clyde was lovely and harmless. But then why had she been told to stay away from him?

'Do you want to come inside?'

Did she? Lola didn't know what she wanted anymore.

Clyde seemed to sense her uneasiness. 'We can sit outside if you like,' he said, gesturing to an old wrought-iron table and matching chairs.

But Lola shook her head and straightened her shoulders. It was time to grow up and stop letting her imagination run away with her.

'No, inside is fine,' she said firmly, and followed him into the shop. Inside it was cool and dusty, cluttered and dark. Chairs and tables were piled up by one wall, a huge chandelier lay on its side in the opposite corner, and a fez hat dangled on a coat rack made out of deer antlers.

'Let's talk,' Clyde said, motioning to a table in the corner of the store. He shuffled off behind a door at the back of the shop, reappearing soon after with a silver tea tray with a teapot and two cups on it.

Lola sat at the table, her hands clasped in her lap.

'Earl Grey tea,' Clyde said, putting the tray down on the table. 'So, it's taken you a long time to stop and look in my window instead of crossing the road. What's changed, if you don't mind me asking?'

'Everything,' said Lola simply. She paused, wondering where on earth she should start. Then she leant forward, her eyes bright. 'Tell me about my mother.'

12

'Your father and mother moved into the cafe over the summer. Your mother was only just pregnant with you. I remember the first time I ever saw her. With her red hair and white skin, she looked like she'd just stepped out of a Dante Rossetti painting. I knew she wouldn't stay here long. Girls like her haven't been prepared for ordinary lives.'

Lola frowned at him, not understanding.

'You see, when you're that beautiful – almost magical to look at – the world offers you different things, and expects different things in return. I've seen it in the theatre. The special ones don't have to wait. They don't have to care. They are forgiven the faults that others are punished for.' Clyde paused, as though he was far away, in another time.

'I wish I could tell you it was hard for her to go, Viola, but I don't know if that's true. She was so young. And I think she was so desperate to be out of the trap her body had caught her in, that as soon as she had you she was already making plans to leave. She was going to London to be an actress in the West End. She would come and sit with me, asking me about my time in the theatre. She would listen for hours to my stories about the plays and the playwrights and the actors.'

Clyde poured them more tea. Lola leant forward, feeling closer to her mother than she could ever remember. Clyde told her how much her mother had loved her, but that she had felt trapped living above a cafe with a small baby she wasn't ready to care for. He told Lola that she had been constantly kissed and adored by her mother.

'So why did she leave then?' asked Lola, wiping away the hot, slow tears.

Even though Clyde's words hurt her, they also soothed her. All she had ever heard was how much she had cried as a baby. To be told that she was loved somehow made it easier and more devastating, all at the same time.

Clyde took a deep breath. 'I don't think she was very well, Lola. She was tired, stressed, she fussed over everything. She would get into these moods. She had such high expectations and she hated herself when she failed to maintain them.'

Lola was silent for a moment as she took this information in.

'Why do Babcia and Dad hate you so much?'

A flash of hurt crossed Clyde face. Lola felt bad for being so candid, but she was sick of tiptoeing around everyone's feelings.

'Because I told them your mother needed help, that she wasn't coping.'

Lola bit the inside of her lip to try and stop the tears, but they wouldn't stop streaming down her face.

'What did they say?' Lola tried to imagine Babcia being told what to do. She knew Babcia's view of modern medicine was bad at the best of times.

'Your grandmother told me to stay away, that I was a bad influence.' His voice was flat, sad. 'We used to be close, your babcia and me. We were great friends. Now she scurries past me as though I did something to make Vivian leave.'

Lola felt sorry for Clyde, sticking his neck out to help a young woman and losing an old friend in the process. She knew how stubborn Babcia could be.

'Your mother told me she was going to leave, but I didn't think she would actually go through with it. Not right then, anyway. She was saying a lot of things that didn't make sense before she left, and I thought she was just creating a fantasy life. And then Delia found you in your pram, with nothing but that note.'

Lola's mouth fell open. She didn't know anything about a note.

'A note?' she whispered, biting the inside of her mouth but hardly tasting the blood. 'What did it say?'

'I don't remember now. You father had it, but maybe he threw it away, or lost it.'

Lola sat in shock. 'Did she tell you where she was going?'

Clyde shook his head slowly. 'She always talked about London, but she never said anything specific. She said she'd write to me, but didn't. I never found out what happened to her, because your babcia hasn't spoken to me since that big fight.' He looked at Lola. 'Can I ask? What did happen to her?'

It was Lola's turn to shake her head. 'I don't know. None of us do. I was going to London. I wanted to at least *try* to find her. But I don't even know what name she uses. I looked on the web and there are at least a hundred Vivian Sanderses in the London area. It would have taken forever to track each one down. And I couldn't find a single Vivian Batko. It was a stupid idea,' she said, realising it for the first time.

Clyde said nothing for a while. 'How is Gisella?' he asked softly.

Lola looked up at Clyde. 'She's good, fine. Annoying,' she added, and then felt disloyal. 'She's Babcia, you know?'

Clyde smiled, and Lola saw a dreamy expression on his face. 'She was always a strong woman.'

Babcia and Clyde? *Oh my god*. Her world really was turning inside out. Lola didn't know what to say, so she stood up to leave. 'Thank you for the tea,' she said warmly. 'Come and see me at the cafe? Life's too short to hang on to old feuds.'

Clyde nodded and bowed a little. 'I'd like that, Miss Lola,' he said, walking Lola to the door.

Don't cry again, she told herself. *Don't cry.*

Lola managed to get through the side door and into the courtyard of the cafe before the outpouring came. She leant into the wall, her face pushed against the rough bricks as she sobbed and sobbed.

She felt movement near her and then a comforting hand on her hair, stroking gently. She lifted her head from the hard bricks, expecting to see Kelsey or Fiona. Instead it was Sam, standing next to her, his face worried.

'Is this because of Babcia?' he asked softly. 'I'm sorry I was being preachy. I should mind my own business.'

Lola shook her head. 'It's not because of that.'

'Then what's up?' he asked, leading her to the overturned milk crates and sitting her down.

Sam held her hand as she cried and buried her head in his shoulder. She missed her dad, she missed her mother, she missed the time when life was simple and she wasn't so tired.

Sam let her cry until she was out of sobs. She pulled away, aware she had left tears and a stain on his shoulder.

'I snotted on you,' she said sadly.

'That's okay, I was hoping to be snotted on today.'

Lola smiled in spite of herself.

'You want to talk yet?'

Lola swallowed, trying to put all the thoughts together in her head. 'I met the old guy who runs the second-hand store up the road. He used to know my mum. He told me some things about her that made me realise how screwed up she was before she left.'

She wiped her eyes on the sleeve of her old T-shirt. 'Everyone always said she was selfish, but she sounded more unwell than selfish.'

'How old was she when she left?'

'Nineteen,' said Lola. 'Only a year older than me.'

'So young to have a baby,' said Sam, shaking his head.

Lola put her head in her hands and sighed. 'I'm glad I didn't go to London to find her now,' she said, looking up at Sam. 'I think that maybe I built her up to be this amazing person, or convinced myself that something mysterious had happened to her. But after talking to Clyde, I think she was just a kid who had a baby and didn't cope.'

'Perhaps.'

'You know, I've always worried about what she would think. Everything I do, I do with the idea that she might come back one day to claim me as her daughter. Like, if I did something amazing then she would come and be proud of me. But the thing is, I never finish anything.'

'Like what?'

'Jobs. Hobbies. I don't work hard and I party a lot. I mean, I'm the fun girl at the party, you know?' Lola picked at the sparkly silver nail polish on her thumb. 'I am like my mother. And if I don't get my shit together I am gonna end up just like her. Running away to find something elusive, and ending up losing the people who love me. I can't be a little girl for the rest of my life. I need to grow up.'

Sam reached out and held her hands in his. 'I think you're being a little hard on yourself.'

'I'll be the sous-chef for the dinner shift, Sam. I'll do whatever it takes to make this cafe work. I'm sick of trying to make my mum proud of me; I want to be proud of myself.'

'You know you're amazing, don't you?' said Sam, his head to one side.

'No I'm not. I'm scatty, unfocused and flighty.'

Sam laughed. 'No, you genuinely don't give a shit what anyone thinks of you, but not in a bad way. You wear what you want, eat how you want, laugh, talk to strangers — you're kind and trusting and a true bohemian. You're great, so don't lose too much of that special Lola flavour.'

It was the nicest Lola summary she had ever heard. She was all those things, really, and she loved that he'd been paying attention. She felt her heart beat a little faster and she noticed how cool his hands were on hers. She remembered the way he had stroked her hair, so gently. God, she was a sucker for her hair being played with. Their eyes met and Lola suddenly wondered what it would be like to kiss him.

And then she saw that Sam had green eyes and snapped out of it. *He has green eyes and a girlfriend*, she told herself.

Lola pulled her hands away and stood up. 'I'll be all right. And thanks for listening.' She paused, trying to gather her thoughts, brushing invisible crumbs from the front of her shorts.

Then she moved past Sam and back to the cafe, where, for the first time in her eighteen years, Lola felt like she had a purpose in life other than to find her mum.

13

The cafe was closed, Lola was visiting her father, and Sam was restless.

He showered, and made himself a croque monsieur. Then he sat with the sandwich and a beer in the living room. He flicked through some of the cookbooks that Lola's dad had obviously collected over the years.

There were hundreds of them in the floor-to-ceiling bookshelf. *It's the dream library for a foodie*, he thought, as he put down his plate and beer and pulled the chair over to stand on.

His hands ran over the books. Some he recognised, some he didn't. Each one beckoned Sam to open them and start to read.

His hand stopped on a blue fabric spine. There was no title

on the spine, so Sam pulled the book out and opened it. A piece of paper fluttered to the floor.

He stepped down from the chair and picked up the note.

Dear David,

I can't help another person live their life until I have lived some of mine first. Clyde will tell you where to get hold of me once I settle in London. Sorry.

Viv

Sam stared at the note and then slipped it inside the front cover and opened up the book.

Inside were pages and pages of handwritten ideas for the cafe. It was obviously David's writing. Some of the ideas were outdated, but some were brilliant and creative. Sam sat down and started to read, his mind whirling with the ideas for food and ambience; the joy that David Batko took in working with food was clear.

Then, a quarter of the way through the book, the writing stopped.

There was nothing in the notebook about why David had stopped writing, but Sam instinctively knew the note from Lola's mother was the reason. He'd stopped dreaming up big ideas for the cafe when Lola's mum left.

Some people can't cook well if their heart is broken, he thought. It was why Sam had left the world of food when Katherine died. For him, great food was made with love, and he was fresh out of supply back then.

Sam checked the note was safe and then closed the book,

returning it to the shelf where he'd found it.

Perhaps some secrets shouldn't be discovered.

Sam sat down on the couch, the ideas from the book whirling in his head. What David had written down thrilled him, and he wondered what it would be like to have his own place one day. The old feeling of excitement flared in his belly. He picked up the pen and pad, covered with hastily scribbled notes, that Lola had left lying on the table.

He crossed out 'offer free wi-fi for customers' from Lola's list — he'd had it installed that morning — and flipped the page. He wrote a list of things he would change if the cafe were his:

- *New breakfast & lunch menus — changing seasonally.*
- *Daily quotes on the menu board — maybe linked to the daily special?*
- *Open for dinner two or three nights a week — Thurs to Sat?*
- *Take-home meals for busy people, including dinners.*

He wrote furiously, one idea leading to another until his hand was cramped. He stopped writing and looked at the list. A realisation slowly came over him as he read.

There's no point in doing any of this, he thought. He threw the disco-ball pen on the table.

He wasn't there to make the cafe his own. He wasn't there to get involved in Lola's life. He was there to get over Katherine, and that was all.

So why had Lola looked at him in the courtyard like she wanted to be kissed? And why did he lie in bed thinking about her?

And why did the note fall from that book as though he was meant to find it?

Had Lola seen it? Did she even know it existed?

Too many questions, thought Sam as he went to bed. But he didn't sleep until he heard Lola come home; and then he finally drifted off.

14

'Dad? Dad, it's Lola.'

'Keep talking to him,' said the recovery nurse, moving wires and cords away so Lola could reach her father's hand. 'It'll help bring him out of the anaesthetic.'

A man in green scrubs approached Lola. 'The operation went well,' he said. 'We've pinned both hips with stabiliser screws to keep the bones aligned. It's all about ensuring the bone regrowth goes according to plan now.'

Lola nodded vaguely, and squeezed her father's hand. It was hard to get a handle on all the medical stuff: screwing things into hips and bones regrowing. She just wanted her dad back.

'He'll spend a week with us,' the surgeon continued, 'and then, all going well, he'll move on to rehabilitation. That's going to take quite a while, I'm sure.'

'How long until he's back on his feet and able to work?'

'It was a severe fracture, on both sides,' the surgeon reminded her. 'I think he's looking at twelve weeks minimum.'

Lola felt her eyes widen.

'It's going to be a lot of hard work for him. It's going to be very painful,' the surgeon said, a little sternly. 'He'll need all the support he can get.'

Lola turned back to her dad and saw him flutter his eyes open.

'Hey, Lollipop,' he said in a groggy voice.

'You did really well,' she said, smiling at him, kissing his forehead. He closed his eyes again, still heavy with the anaesthetic.

By the time her dad was settled in his room and she had spoken to Babcia, Lola was desperate to get back to the cafe.

She left the hospital and, seeing her bus pulling into the stop ahead, ran for it. She just managed to jump on board before the driver closed the doors and pulled out into the traffic. *I have to get my licence*, she thought as she fell, out of breath, onto a seat.

As the bus moved slowly through the streets Lola stared out the window, watching the city pass her by: people busily crossing streets, sitting at cafes, talking on their phones. A red-headed woman crossed the road and Lola glanced back at her, just to make sure. *The curse of the missing red-headed mother,* she thought. She wondered if she'd ever be able to kick the habit of scanning the streets for her mum.

Lola stood up and glanced at her reflection in the bus window. Her red hair looked wild with the sunlight shining though the flyaway hairs.

She shouldn't look so scruffy, what with her role running the cafe. She should be more serious, like a businesswoman, in cute, fitted knee-length skirts and crisp white shirts. Or sensible, like Jane – minus the daggy jumpers.

Oh, who am I kidding? she thought as she got off the bus at her stop. She was never going to be serious about the way she looked. Her hair was her crown of crazy, and maybe that was okay. She walked down the street towards the cafe.

As she approached, she saw Sam standing out the front on the street. He waved at her. She smiled. Sam was her friend now, she realised as she waved back. He was such a lovely guy. It was a shame he would be off on his travels when her dad eventually came back.

Shame he had a girlfriend.

Lola had never been with a boy who had a girlfriend, and she would never let it happen, no matter what her feelings were. She had often discussed this with her girlfriends, and they'd all agreed they'd never do it. Don't want it to happen to you? Then don't do it to anyone else. Lola's loyalty to the sisterhood was fierce.

The cafe was nearly full as she stepped in, possibly thanks to their new free wi-fi. Writerly types and students with their laptops sat at tables, intent on their work – or Facebook.

The new crowd gave the cafe a younger, more relaxed vibe

that Lola liked. She picked up an empty coffee cup and plate as she walked past a table.

'That was a great lunch,' she heard, and she looked down to see a handsome face staring up at her.

'Oh yeah?' She flirted a little. 'What did you have?'

'The pide special,' the man replied, and she felt him looking her up and down.

She smiled. 'Good choice. Can I get you another coffee?'

He was older, maybe twenty-five, with deep brown eyes. His forearms were tanned and strong, and he was wearing a fancy-looking watch. His T-shirt was expensive-looking, his jeans designer.

He wasn't her type, but then who was? Sam, who had a girl-friend back in England?

'No, I don't want a coffee,' he replied seriously. 'But I *would* love your number. Would you have a drink with me?'

Lola couldn't help but be impressed by his confidence. 'I don't have drinks with men whose names I don't know,' she said firmly, but she knew her eyes were sparkling.

'Andrew.' He put his hand out for Lola to shake, but she gestured to the items in her hands. She shrugged lightly and walked to the kitchen.

'Who's the hottie?' Fiona burst out as she followed Lola into the kitchen.

'Andrew,' said Lola, and she noticed Sam turning away from the bacon he was frying to see what the fuss was about.

'He's feckin' gorgeous,' said Fiona. 'You should give him your number. Or mine. Either or.' She dumped the plates she was carrying and headed back to the cafe.

'You can't go out with a customer,' said Sam, turning back to his now-overcooked bacon. 'Shit,' he said, throwing it out and grabbing a new batch to cook.

Lola looked at him and laughed. 'Who are you, my dad?' She walked out into the cafe, scribbling her name and number on her order pad and putting it on the table in front of Andrew.

'Call me, maybe?' she said with a flick of her hair, not knowing if Sam was watching but sort of hoping he was.

Andrew looked down at the paper. 'Lola.' He smiled sexily.

'It's short for Viola,' she said.

'Imagine if your name was Lynn and you said it was short for Violin,' he said, chuckling. Lola stared at him, instantly regretting giving him her number. What a dumb joke. Out of the corner of her eye she saw Sam spying on her through the servery window, so she laughed.

'Good one,' she said, putting her hand on Andrew's arm. 'I look forward to the call.'

She moved through the cafe as though on skates, picking up dirty dishes and talking to customers as Andrew paid the bill.

And when he left, she saw him watching her through the window.

Be kind, Lola reminded herself. He might not be a total dickhead, but honestly? That joke wasn't a great start.

For the rest of the shift Sam was sulky, which Lola thought was funny. Even Kelsey and Fiona picked up on it.

'He's got his knickers in a twist about something,' said Kelsey as they packed up for the day.

Lola watched as Sam thumped about the kitchen. She felt mean until she remembered she hadn't done anything wrong. Wasn't it Sam who had the girlfriend, after all?

⁓

The next morning when Lola woke, sweat was running down her neck. She stretched in her bed. Her muscles ached and her mouth was dry.

'Ahhh,' she moaned, keeping her eyes closed. She wasn't quite ready to face the day.

Dreams about her mother always messed with her head. Whenever she dreamed about her mum, she was certain to have a bad day. It was one of her superstitions, just like Babcia's one about people with green eyes.

Last night's dream was the same as always; for as long as she could remember, she'd had this dream. Lola was on one side of a river, her mum on the other. Lola could never get her mum's attention. She'd frantically wave and call out, but her mum never responded. Eventually her mother would walk away, leaving a sobbing Lola on the other side of the river.

Maybe it was the heat, thought Lola. After an underwhelming summer the previous night had been stiflingly hot, and today was going to be a scorcher. At least the cafe has air conditioning, she thought, as she rolled out of bed and did the only yoga she knew, the salute to the sun.

There was a knock at her door. 'Come in,' she called from her downward dog pose.

Sam stood in the doorway, dressed and ready for work.

'Morning,' she said, looking up at him while trying to maintain her pose.

'What are you doing?'

'Yoga.'

'Why?' He looked at her as though she was hanging upside down from the roof.

'Because I had shitty dreams and this helps. What do you want?' Lola lowered herself onto her hands and knees and looked at Sam properly. 'You're messing with my Zen.'

'There's no water,' he announced.

'What?' Lola stood up and ran past Sam. In the bathroom she tried turning on the tap. Nothing came out. 'Shit,' she said, racing back into her room and grabbing her phone. She dialled quickly and cursed under her breath when the call went straight to voicemail.

'Hi, Jane? It's Lola. I know it's early, but the water's gone off and I don't know if it's because of the bill. When is the extension till? Call me back.' Lola hung up and raised her eyebrows at Sam. 'Fun times at Cafe Ambrosia, huh?'

She and Sam sat on her bedroom floor, waiting for Jane to return the call. Within a few minutes Jane called back.

'Jane rang the water company. The whole block is out,' said Lola with relief after hanging up. 'It's not just us. Apparently it'll be back on soon.'

Sam nodded. 'Kind of makes it hard to make coffee and tea though, doesn't it?'

Lola stood, deep in thought. 'Maybe. Let me get dressed and I'll meet you downstairs.'

Lola pushed Sam out the door, pulled off her boxer shorts and Snoopy T-shirt and pulled on underwear, denim shorts and her tank top with tropical fruits on the front. She put a bandana around her head and slipped on her Converse before bounding down the stairs.

Kelsey and Fiona had arrived and were in the kitchen, looking concerned.

'At least the new cafe can't serve coffees either,' Fiona was saying to Sam and Kelsey.

'Oi, no gloomy faces. I have an idea,' Lola said.

All three looked up at her.

'You look cute,' Fiona said.

Lola laughed. 'Thanks, but who cares what I look like? We have to make some money today and here's how we're going to do it.' She clapped her hands excitedly. 'You know we have that huge thingy of coffee in the coolroom, for the tiramisu?'

They nodded.

'Well, since we have no water until god knows when, and it's going to be a stinker of a day, I suggest we offer iced coffee and coffee granitas. We can make it with the ice blocks in the coolroom and the ice shaver.'

'We could serve *mazagrans*,' said Fiona excitedly.

'What's that?' asked Kelsey.

'It's a cold drink I got addicted to in Portugal when I was there last year. It's espresso, lemon, ice and sugar.'

'Great,' said Lola. 'Anything else?'

'Iced chocolates and iced cappuccinos would work too, with shaved chocolate on top,' offered Kelsey.

'Love it. Let's get organised. Fiona, you write the drinks menu on the board. Kelsey, check we have enough supplies in the coolroom.' Lola looked at Sam and made a face. 'God, what a disaster,' she sighed.

'I think you're doing beautifully,' he said. 'Very efficient and just the right amount of bossy.'

'Ha,' laughed Lola, knowing she was blushing a little.

'And Fiona is right, you do look awfully cute today,' he added, looking away.

Lola frowned. That was definitely flirting. 'Are you flirting with me?' she asked, her eyebrows raised and her hands on her hips. 'Don't you have a girlfriend?'

Sam looked flustered and was about to speak when Lola heard the bell above the door signalling that a caffeine-craving commuter had arrived. She moved quickly from the kitchen before

Sam could say anything.

As each customer came in, Lola explained that the water was out and that they could only offer cold drinks. Not many people were discouraged by the news and soon the orders were rolling in. Lola rushed in and out of the kitchen, helping Kelsey and Fiona. Sam made easy toasted sandwiches and bircher muesli for those who wanted food, but Lola refused to make the kitchen any more frantic and stopped him from making more complicated breakfast items. To her surprise people were fine with the change, with a few even asking if they were always going to serve the iced coffees.

'Thank god you're open. The cafe around the corner is shut and if I don't get my espresso I'm a bitch all day,' said one woman, who Lola had never seen before.

'You know it's going to be served cold?' asked Lola, gesturing to the menu.

'Oh, that's fine with me, as long as I get my fix,' laughed the woman.

As the morning wore on the water still wasn't connected and they had run out of coffee, so by lunchtime Lola decided to call it a day.

'Go home,' she said to the girls. 'We're done. We did better than I thought we would,' she added, as she balanced up the till.

Fiona and Kelsey swept and mopped the floor and then left Lola counting the money and filling in the bank slip. Sam stood in the kitchen doorway.

'Hectic morning,' he said.

'Yep,' said Lola, not looking up as she counted twenty-cent pieces.

'We did okay though, I think.'

She nodded, concentrating.

'About before —' Sam started.

'Shhhh, I'll lose count,' Lola interrupted crossly.

Sam turned and walked back into the kitchen. She could hear him noisily banging pots and pans about.

'Christ,' she muttered to herself and, grabbing the money, walked into the kitchen and dumped it on the bench. 'What?' she snapped at Sam.

'I wanted to say that when I said you looked cute before, I wasn't flirting. I was merely agreeing with what Fiona said.'

'Okay,' said Lola, feeling stung.

They paused and looked at each other.

'I just don't think it would be right for us to have something happen when we live together and you work here,' said Lola with a shrug of her shoulders.

'Fair enough,' said Sam easily, as he leant back against the bench.

'And you have a girlfriend,' Lola added, which was the real truth of the matter.

Sam swallowed and looked down at his feet. The look of shame, thought Lola.

'About that . . .' Sam trailed off.

'What? You suddenly broke up? How convenient,' Lola laughed bitterly.

Sam shook his head. 'No . . . actually . . . she died.'

Lola froze, unsure if he was joking. If he was, it wasn't very funny. 'When? Just in the last week?' she said lightly.

His green eyes bore into her with such intensity she felt herself draw back.

'She died over a year ago. Blood clot in the brain. We were engaged.' He paused, swallowed. 'She was everything to me.' His face was emotionless, his voice doing all the work for him. 'That's why I'm travelling. Or running away, I suppose.'

Lola didn't know what to say. She didn't know anyone who had died. And she didn't know anyone who was engaged either. It all seemed very grown-up and really sad, and her heart broke a little. All this talk of her problems, when he was dealing with this?

'I'm really sorry,' said Lola. 'For your loss — and for her loss. I'm sure she's bloody pissed off that it ended up like this.'

Sam laughed, and the tone in the kitchen lifted. 'Oh yeah, she would be well pissed off.' He looked at Lola and smiled. 'We had so many plans.'

'I'm sure you did.'

'Maybe I *was* flirting with you before,' he admitted sheepishly. 'I'm not very good at it.'

'That's okay. I appreciate the compliment.' Lola's head was spinning as she thought all this through. 'But why did you say you had a girlfriend?'

'To make you feel better about me moving in.'

Lola nodded slowly.

'I take it you don't really have a boyfriend?' Sam ventured.

Lola shook her head.

'So I guess we both lied.' Sam smiled sadly. 'But you're right, it's better we don't start anything that we can't finish properly.' He pushed off the bench and untied his apron. 'Well, if that's it for the day, I'm going to head down to the beach. Want to come?'

The kitchen felt warmer than it had a few minutes ago. Lola picked up the banking paraphernalia and stuffed it under her arm.

'No thanks. We redheads aren't designed for the beach, and I have to go and see Dad.'

Taking the keys for the back door, she headed outside and locked the back gate behind her.

A dead girlfriend. A made-up boyfriend. No water and a heat wave. Lola mused over it all as she walked towards the bank. *And I thought I had to go overseas to find adventure?*

Nope, Babcia was right. If you stood still long enough, crazy would find you.

15

Sam didn't know why he'd told Lola about Katherine. He thought about it all afternoon at the beach. He didn't owe Lola anything more than gratitude for the job, yet he had wanted her to know. But why?

Finally, he decided it was the way she had looked at him, as though he was cheating pond scum. He had never cheated and never would. He wanted her to know this — but again, he wasn't sure why it was so important.

There was obviously an attraction between them, but maybe it was nothing more than sexual energy — the sort that might drive a one-night stand. Not that Sam had had any of those, either before or after Katherine. He'd only ever been with women that he wanted to spend more time with. He could never understand wanting to be with someone like that, and then wanting to walk away from them the next morning.

On the way home from the beach he bought a few beers for himself and Lola. He loved hanging out with her upstairs at night, with her jumping from one topic to another, playing her favourite songs for him on her laptop and telling him her crazy ideas about life. Lola's energy was so infectious. He doubted so many people would have ordered cold coffees today without Lola's charm. She was born to work front of house in a restaurant.

Sam unlatched the back gate and walked inside and up the stairs, where he could hear loud music playing.

'Hello?' he called.

Music was a good sign. It probably meant she was in a good mood. Not sulking about him lying to her, anyway. He pondered this as he sat down, cracked open two beers and set them on the table. A peace offering, maybe.

'I didn't hear you come in,' he heard, and looked up to see Lola in the hallway. 'Water's back on.'

She had plaited her hair and pinned it up, so it circled her head like a crown, a bit Princess Leia–like. She was wearing a red checked dress with strawberries on it, and red ballet flats. Some red lipstick completed the outfit. Sam thought he had never seen anyone look so delicious.

'You like clothes with fruits on them,' he said, remembering her tropical-fruit singlet from earlier in the day. He'd tried to avoid looking at her singlet too closely all morning.

'What can I say? I'm fruitilicious.' Lola gave a small curtsy.

'Want a beer?' He lifted his own to his lips, finding his mouth suddenly dry.

'Oh, no thanks. I'm going out,' she said, turning on her heel and heading back into her room.

Sam sat still, wondering where she was going. Then wondering what made him think it was any of his business.

Lola walked out again, digging for something in a little yellow handbag.

'How's your dad?' he asked.

'Okay, considering. He's on a drip for pain relief so whenever he feels pain he presses this pump thing. Babcia was there today and every time she spoke, I swear he pumped it.'

'Ha,' said Sam, though he didn't feel like laughing. 'Where you off to?'

'Just out with a friend,' said Lola vaguely.

Sam realised she had a date. 'Have fun,' he said, the words sounding fake even to his own ears.

Lola walked to the top of the stairs. 'I'd invite you, but it's a small thing,' she said. Sam was pretty sure her cheeks flushed with the lie.

'No really, it's fine. Go.'

Sam was soon alone. He stretched out on the sofa and put his hands above his head. *Bloody hell*, he thought. *What a mess*. He drained his beer and then the beer meant for Lola.

Then he showered and changed. There was only one thing for it, he decided. It was time to get pissed.

He had never been much of a drinker, unlike most of his friends back home. He didn't have time to drink; he worked most nights, and when all the others clocked off and hit the pub, Sam had always wanted to race home and curl up next to Katherine's warm, sleepy body.

Now Sam wanted to drink and escape the girls invading his mind. The ghost of Katherine, trailing him at every turn. And Lola, unknowingly taunting him with her incredible energy, her crazy hair and her cute smile.

Sam left the cafe, walked down the street and took the bus into town. He knew where the backpackers liked to drink and headed there, walking among the crowds of office workers leaving for the day. Soon he found the pub and, as he opened the old doors, a cacophony of drunken accents greeted him. British, German, Scandinavian, American, French.

Crossing the floor to the bar, he ordered a pint of Guinness, drank it quickly and ordered another. By his third beer he was chatting to a group of Swedes, who were insisting he travel with them to pick fruit up north. On his fourth beer he found himself friends with an Irish guy who reckoned he knew the meaning of life, and that he had seen God at the top of Mount Kilimanjaro.

By the time he'd poured his heart out to a pretty Norwegian girl, who had responded to his pain by taking him to the bathroom and making out with him until his mouth hurt, he'd lost count of the beers.

'Let's go back to your place,' she said in her heavy accent, pulling him towards her.

'Not tonight, sorry,' he slurred, kissing her cheek and stepping out of the pub and into the warm night.

Sam somehow found his way back to the cafe and, after staggering up the stairs, he saw that Lola's bedroom door was open – she wasn't home yet. He started singing 'Lola' by The Kinks as he tried to undress. He fell against the wall, bouncing off it and into her bedroom.

He stopped singing and tried to focus on not stepping on the mess of shoes, clothes and papers spread across the floor.

'Christ, she's messy,' he muttered as he stood on a hairbrush. He fell onto her unmade bed and buried his face in her pillow. He fell asleep humming 'Lola'.

~

Sam woke up to a cruel splash of cold water on his face.

'Get up, dickhead,' he heard.

He moaned. Why would she wake him in the middle of the night? 'What's the time?' he mumbled, his tongue not doing what it usually did when he tried to speak.

'Six,' Lola replied.

'Did you have to throw water at me?' he asked. God, his head hurt. He debated whether or not he needed to throw up.

'I've been trying to wake you up for fifteen minutes.'

Sam finally opened his eyes properly. Lola was still dressed in last night's clothes, and was holding an empty bottle of water. Sam moaned and sat up, realising he was in his red briefs and white sports socks. Then he remembered the Norwegian girl from the pub and groaned. Could this get any worse?

'What? Are you gonna spew? You better not spew in my room,' said Lola crossly.

Sam stood up without answering and gingerly made his way to the bathroom where he turned on the shower, hoping it would wash at least some of his shame away.

No doubt Lola will give me my marching orders now, he thought as he dried himself. Certainly she wouldn't want him living there anymore, but would she even want him in the kitchen? He might have to resign himself to unemployment. Maybe he'd be picking fruit up north after all.

He dressed and went downstairs, where Lola was already setting up the tables and chairs outside. He set to work, prepping for breakfast, as Lola walked back in and put something on the bench. He looked down and saw two aspirins and a glass of water.

Lola smiled. 'I figured you might need these.'

Sam popped the pills immediately, taking a big swig of water to get them down. If only they could make his head stop hurting, then he might get through the morning. 'You're not going to fire me?'

'Fire you? For getting pissed?'

'But I slept in your bed.'

'Did you go through my things?'

'No.'

'Did you try on my underwear?'

'No!'

'Did you have a wank in my bed?'

'What? No! Jesus, Lola.'

'Then we're fine,' said Lola archly, as Fiona and Kelsey walked in.

'How was the date?' asked Fiona, as soon as she saw Lola.

Lola shrugged and Sam turned back to the Roma tomatoes he was grilling.

'You know, fine. He's quite nice.'

'What does he do?' asked Kelsey.

'He's in the food industry. He's, er, a rep for a coffee company. No-one I'd heard of.'

'Oh wow, he must have liked what you've done with the cafe,' said Fiona proudly.

Sam chopped herbs with more concentration than usual. Firstly, because he wanted Lola to keep talking, but secondly because he was aware his coordination wasn't what it should be. He just needed to survive this awful day, ideally without losing any fingers.

'I didn't tell him it was Dad's. I just said I was a waitress,' she said. 'I honestly didn't want to go into the hassle of everything that has happened. I just wanted a fun night out, you know?'

Fiona and Kelsey murmured in agreement as they followed Lola into the cafe.

Sam put the knife down. *A coffee rep*, he thought. *A wanker who probably teaches baristas how to create 'coffee art' with the froth.*

All morning Lola acted like nothing had happened. When the lunchtime rush was finally over and the others were cleaning up, she wandered into the kitchen.

'What's happening?' she asked, picking up a mango and sniffing it.

'Just trying to stay alive,' said Sam, 'with the worst headache of all time.'

'Still?' asked Lola.

Sam gave her a look that obviously told Lola everything, because she walked into the coolroom and returned with a can of Coke.

'One can of black aspirin,' she said, putting it front of him.

Sam opened it and took a sip. He didn't normally drink Coke, but Lola was right. He definitely felt better with all that sugar coursing through his veins.

Lola took the mango and a small knife and peeled it over the sink, eating it greedily, sucking and slurping the flesh as Sam watched her, a little horrified but also intrigued.

'What?' she looked up at him, her face covered in mango juice.

'Enjoying that?'

Lola went back to her mango and was soon sucking the last bits of flesh from the pip.

He was pretty sure Lola didn't realise he was getting turned on watching her, which made it even sexier. *Bloody hell*, he thought, *how hung-over am I?*

He was getting turned on by fruit.

16

The truth was that Lola's date with Andrew had been a disaster. It had started badly when she first met him at the bar and he casually commented that she wasn't really dressed up enough for the restaurant he had planned to take her to.

Instead of offering to go home and change, Lola stood her ground. She liked her dress and felt good in it.

The bar he'd chosen was the kind of place where everyone was desperately trying to prove how cool they were. Andrew had high-fived the bartender when ordering. Lola had tried not to show her dismay. *Not a high-fiver*, she thought, as she ordered a pink lemonade cocktail.

Andrew had turned up his nose at her order. 'Really?'

'Really,' said Lola firmly.

So far he didn't like her drink choice or her dress. And they were, what, five minutes into the date? *Well, too bad*, she decided. But the worst was still to come.

It was pretty clear she had made a mistake in saying yes when Andrew asked her out. She had said yes because he'd looked at her in a way that made her feel sexy and pretty and fun. She had almost forgotten what it was like to be fun; since her dad's accident she had been feeling so boring and responsible.

Andrew was cute and sexy, and the date should have been fun. But as she sat opposite him, she realised suddenly that she hadn't wanted him to ask her out. She had wanted Sam to ask her out. To flirt and take her number and call her within ten minutes of leaving with plans for that night. Except that they lived together. But still.

Lola hadn't told Andrew about her dad or Sam or her trip away. She'd wanted to be normal for a night, the fun girl with no cares or worries. So she told him she was going to wait tables for a year.

'Do you like it at the cafe?'

'Sure, it's fine,' Lola had replied vaguely.

'They've made a few changes recently, I see,' Andrew said, sipping his twelve-dollar beer.

Lola nodded.

'I own a cafe,' Andrew said casually. 'It's the one around the corner, Blueberry. You heard of it?'

Lola's blood ran cold. 'Yeah, I have.'

'You probably read our review in the paper. It's been great for us. The guy who wrote it is a mate of mine. Did me a favour.'

'That's lucky,' said Lola carefully.

Easy, Lola, she told herself, *don't run at him with guns blazing just yet. Wait.*

'Actually, I'm looking for staff and people have been saying how great your new chef is,' Andrew said. 'Do you think he'd like a job with me? I mean, you can come too, of course. I can always do with another waitress.'

It took every ounce of self-control — something that Lola didn't have much of — for her not to throw her drink at him. But that would have been a waste — it was a very nice drink.

'No, he wouldn't be interested,' she snapped. 'He's going travelling again soon.'

'Shame,' Andrew said, leaning back in his chair. 'But what about you? Maybe you could give me a little incentive to give you the best shifts.'

'Oh really?' asked Lola, trying not to laugh at him now. The night was becoming more and more bizarre. 'You want me to sleep with you so you'll give me primo shifts at your shitty cafe?'

Andrew's face turned stony. 'It's not shitty. Not like that coffee-serving op shop you work in.'

'Don't you dare say that,' she hissed, surprised at how angry she was.

'Listen, I'm gonna ruin that cafe. Sooner or later it'll have to close, and you'll be begging me for a job.'

Lola drained the dregs of her pink lemonade and then stood up. She did the only thing she could think of. She leant over close to him, as though she was going to kiss him. So close . . . and then she pulled his designer shirt away from his toned chest and poured the ice down his front.

'You stupid bitch!' he yelped as he ripped the bottom of his shirt out of his jeans and let the ice fall onto the floor.

Lola turned and walked out of the bar, adrenaline coursing through her body. It was the most satisfying moment she'd had in ages and she grinned all the way to the bus stop.

But what to do? If she went home she knew what would probably happen. She would kiss Sam, maybe even take him into her bedroom. And then it would be weird and awkward the next morning.

The most grown-up thing to do was to leave Sam alone. It wasn't just about what Lola wanted anymore, it was about what she needed to do to keep things running smoothly. The sum of the whole, or whatever the expression was.

She checked her phone and saw it was still early, so she went to visit her dad. Lola was surprised to see Jane there. Jane in a red windcheater with a pirate parrot appliquéd on the front. It even had an eye patch and a gold earring.

Lola noticed her father seemed embarrassed, so she didn't stay long.

Then she rang Toby, her on-and-off-again ex-boyfriend. He was usually a sure thing. Except he wasn't a sure thing anymore.

He had a new girlfriend. Over the phone he told her he was sorry to hear about her dad, he liked her dad. *Hell, who doesn't*, thought Lola.

Then she tried Rosie and Sarah, who she discovered had gone to Rosie's parents' beach house – without asking Lola. She couldn't have gone, of course, but that didn't stop it from pissing her off.

Then Babcia rang, and Lola had a distraction for the evening. Babcia was so pleased that Lola came for dinner that she wouldn't let her go home.

'It's too late now. You stay,' she insisted.

And Lola realised she was stuck for the night. But it was okay; Babcia was in fine form, and Lola even gently tried to question her about Clyde and his shop.

'Why wasn't I allowed to go to that antique shop when I was a kid, Babcia?'

'I don't remember,' Babcia said quickly, not looking at Lola as she cleared the dishes.

'I'm sure you could if you tried.'

'Some things aren't vorth remembering.' Her words seemed so final, Lola decided to let it go . . . for now.

Babcia woke Lola early so she could get to work. She offered to come and help at the cafe for the day, but Lola swiftly deflected her offer and instead sent her on a mission to buy David new toiletries for the move to the rehab centre the next day.

Lola had arrived at the cafe before six, surprised to see the kitchen light wasn't on, and that Sam wasn't up and prepping yet.

That's when she found him in her bed. What the hell was he doing there? The covers were kicked off, and he was all lean and sexy in the rumpled sheets.

She tried to wake him, but quickly decided he probably deserved the water treatment. He was obviously hung-over. It was funny to watch Sam struggle with his hangover all morning; clearly he wasn't a big drinker.

It was also fun to watch his reaction to the girls asking about her date. But then she felt bad. She shouldn't mess with Sam — not only for the cafe's sake, but also because he was fragile.

He isn't ready for anything yet, not even fun, she thought, as she showered after the cafe closed that day. Once, she wouldn't have worried about his feelings, she would have just pushed her way into his life and bed if that was what she wanted. Now, as she dried herself and looked in the mirror, Lola saw what she had become. She was finally a grown-up.

17

'We need to start opening for dinner, like you suggested,' said Lola, her hair wrapped in a turban, as she walked out of her bedroom wearing a Japanese kimono over denim shorts and a tank top.

Sam was going through the shelf of cookbooks.

'Not tonight, I hope,' he said as he lay down on the sofa, pulling a cushion over his head. 'I'm knackered.'

His T-shirt rode up, revealing his stomach, and Lola had a sudden urge to tickle it. Usually she acted on her urges, but in this instance she wasn't sure it was a good idea. She was Sam's boss, after all.

Instead she flipped her head over and unwound the towel, water dripping on the floor.

'How's the hangover?'

'I'm just tired now. I need to go to bed early.'

'Just make sure you hop into your own bed tonight, Goldilocks.' She sat on the armchair and looked at her toenails. She needed a pedicure but she didn't have the time or energy to do one — she didn't really have time to do anything but work these days. And yet she wasn't upset to realise this. She actually kind of liked it.

'So, dinners,' she said. 'We should go and find somewhere nice, see how they do things. You know, steal some ideas.'

Sam didn't say anything from under the pillow.

'Sam?'

'What?'

'Do you want to go out for dinner?'

'Now?' he moaned.

'Yeah, come on.'

If they went out in public, then she wouldn't be here, with Sam tempting her with his lean cuteness and smooth, toned stomach. They could talk business, it would get late, and they could sleep in their own beds, without her urges getting the better of her.

Sam reluctantly sat up and threw the cushion at her.

'You're a tough boss,' he said. He stood up and headed to his room to change.

Lola changed into the dress she had worn the night before and quickly dried off her hair enough to tie it into a topknot. She didn't wear much make-up, just mascara, lip gloss and perfume.

'Come on, slowcoach,' she called from the hallway.

Sam opened the door, looking slightly fresher in a blue shirt with rolled-up sleeves.

'Nice shirt,' she said cheekily.

'Thanks, it's your dad's,' he admitted.

'I know, I ironed it.'

'I like that dress,' he said, as they started walking down the stairs. 'I was going to say something last night but you rushed out the door before I could.'

Behind Sam on the stairs, unseen, Lola threw up her hands in frustration. What were the gods thinking, taunting her like this? She'd always been a sucker for a compliment, if it was sincere, like Sam's clearly was.

Sam was oblivious. 'Where are we headed? Do you have a car?'

'No car,' she said. 'But I am planning to get my licence and save up for one.'

'Then we'll get the bus,' he said, and they walked towards the bus stop.

'Let's just see where the night takes us, shall we? I want an adventure. If we see a place we like, then we'll stop there.'

'What about,' said Sam, looking enthused suddenly, 'we go to different places for entree, main and dessert?'

'I love it,' said Lola, so loudly that people turned to look at them. 'You're a freaking genius.' She pushed Sam in the chest.

'And you're nuts,' he laughed, rubbing his chest where she had poked him.

A bus trundled up and the doors hissed open.

Lola touched her bus pass to the reader, then she walked down to the back of the bus and sat down.

'I should have known you'd be a back-seat rebel,' Sam said, sitting down next to her.

'You'd be surprised. I'm not as naughty as people assume,' said Lola. 'I think it's the red hair. People think I'm trouble. Red hair has a lot to answer for, you know.'

Sam laughed. 'You also don't seem to give a shit about much.'

'Ha,' said Lola, wagging her finger at him. 'That's where my scheming is so brilliant. You see, I do give a shit about lots of things. A very big shit.' Sam made a face and Lola laughed. 'Okay, bad use of words. What I mean is, I do care about people. And about life. I just don't worry about a lot of the things other people do. And I never worry about what people think of me.'

'That's unusual,' mused Sam. 'I thought all girls worried about that.'

'Did Katherine worry about what people thought of her?' asked Lola, glancing at him.

Sam flinched and Lola hoped it was okay to mention her. She hadn't planned to; it had just come out.

'I suppose so,' he said, looking out the window. 'She worried about what people thought about us getting married so young.'

'Did you?'

'Nope, ' he said firmly. 'I knew she was the girl for me, it's no-one else's business'

Lola stared ahead, her good mood deflated. She knew she was being silly. Was she really jealous of a dead girl? And did she actually expect to replace the love of his life after a few weeks of working in a kitchen together?

They were quiet for the rest of the bus trip to the city. They sat on the back seat, a space between them as though The Ghost of Girlfriend Past was sitting there. *Which in a way*, thought Lola, *she is*.

'Let's get off here,' said Lola. She pressed the button and stood up, swinging a little with the rhythm of the bus as she walked towards the front, Sam following. She held on to the overhead rail and was suddenly aware her dress was very short when her arm was above her head. She felt cheap all of a sudden, as though she was trying to turn Sam on.

Hurriedly, she moved to the front door of the bus and waited, holding the upright steel pole so her dress didn't ride up again. She heard Sam move behind her, and then his hand closed above hers on the pole. She turned to see he was right behind her, so close. She leant back, so slightly, just enough to let him know she knew.

What it was she was supposed to know, she couldn't quite put her finger on. But she knew there was something going on, and that he felt it too. They climbed off the bus and onto the street, turning to face each other.

'I like you,' Sam said simply, with a small shrug.

Lola's eyes searched his face, settling on his green eyes. 'I know.'

'I like you a lot.'

'You work for me,' she said, blinking.

'I know. And I'm still a bit screwed up.'

'I know.'

'Be patient with me?'

'I'll try.'

And then Lola went on her tiptoes and kissed him on the forehead. 'Let's just be friends for now, then?'

Sam nodded. 'Probably for the best.'

They walked up the street towards a collection of bars and restaurants. It was warm and there were people having after-work drinks and couples holding hands and families milling around.

'This is a pretty touristy part of the city,' Lola explained as they walked. 'But I like it. By the river it's always happy, it makes me feel good to be here.'

They stood and watched a fire-eater on stilts and his sidekick juggling chainsaws, with a huge crowd around them. Sam laughed at their antics and Lola found herself glancing at him a few times. When he relaxed he was really cute. But sometimes, like before on the bus, his face was a study of pain and loss. When he was like that he was almost hard to look at. The grief must have been horrible to live with, she imagined.

They found a funky modern Mexican restaurant for entree. They ordered two serves of tacos – one with black beans and one with beef and chorizo.

'Mexico is so hot right now,' said Lola, as she watched the busy waiters move across the tiled floor.

'I would imagine so, but isn't Mexico always hot?'

'I mean the food,' laughed Lola. 'It's super huge here. Taco trucks and bar menus and restaurants. Everyone's loco about Mexico.'

Sam nodded and they ate their tacos, concentrating on the textures and flavours.

'That was good,' said Sam, as they paid and left the restaurant in search of their main course. 'I get why it's so popular. It's fun to eat, great flavours and not expensive.'

'Should we do something Mexican?' Lola mused, as they stood outside an Italian restaurant.

'Let's eat here,' said Sam, opening the door for Lola.

There were no tables left, but there were seats at the bar. As Sam surveyed the wine list, Lola felt conspicuous in her summer dress. 'I don't think I'm dressed up enough,' she whispered as she looked around at the well-dressed patrons and the bow-tied waitstaff.

Sam glanced at her and frowned. 'I thought you didn't care what people thought.'

Lola shrugged. 'I just feel like I'm being disrespectful by not dressing up. I do like to dress up sometimes, you know.'

'For what it's worth, I think you look lovely. Now, what will you order?'

Lola tried to focus on the menu but the urge to kiss Sam was so strong she thought she might fall backwards off the stool, taking him with her. Or she might fall on top of him. Either would be fine. Instead she sighed and straightened up. 'What looks good?'

'Maybe the *linguine di mare al cartoccio*,' said Sam in what sounded like perfect Italian to Lola.

'Huh?'

'It's seafood. All the good bits, like prawns and mussels, baked in parchment paper with a fresh tomato sauce.'

Lola nodded. It sounded perfect to her.

'And I'll have the *pappardelle al guanciale e barolo*.'

'Now you're showing off,' laughed Lola.

As the waiter behind the bar came over, Sam ordered their meals and two glasses of wine.

'We have to have wine,' he said.

'Even with your nasty hangover?'

Sam nodded in mock seriousness. 'I feel ready.'

Their meals were fantastic. Lola was just settling the bill when she saw Sam waving at someone in the far corner of the restaurant.

'Who is it?' she asked, surprised that he knew someone.

'It's Babcia.'

'Who?' Lola looked at him, confused. She must have misheard. She peered around Sam and saw Babcia sitting with Clyde at a cosy corner table.

18

'Oh my god,' said Lola under her breath as she walked towards the table. 'Babcia?'

Both faces turned to her, embarrassed, and Lola felt like a mother catching her daughter out on an unauthorised date. She was extremely glad she'd made Sam wait outside while she went to talk to them.

'I rang Gisella after we spoke,' explained Clyde, looking completely delighted. 'I thought it was time we let go of the past.'

Babcia nodded furiously in agreement. 'Ve used to be good friends,' she said. 'And then things became difficult.'

The reason for their estrangement hung in the air.

Clyde was wearing a suit and pink polka-dotted tie. Babcia was in her good black dress with the enamel brooch Lola had given her for her birthday last year. She even had a little blue eye shadow on.

It seemed Lola and her dad weren't the only ones whose lives had changed completely when her mother disappeared.

'Have a gorgeous night,' said Lola warmly, kissing Babcia on the cheek.

She met Sam outside the door.

'Who was Babcia's date?' he asked.

'The man up the road. The one who owns the antique shop,' said Lola as they started walking. 'He was the one who told me about a note in my pram when my mother abandoned me.'

'What did the note say?'

'He said he couldn't remember,' said Lola, wondering for the first time if that was actually true.

'Still want to get dessert somewhere?' asked Sam, his body language indicating his uncertainty about what to do now.

'I don't think I could do the sit-down thing again,' admitted Lola. 'I'm a bit spun out.'

'That's okay,' he said, leading her to a seat by the river. 'Stay here and wait for me?'

Lola nodded and watched a party boat go by. It was filled with people about her age, laughing and singing without a care in the world. What were they celebrating? An eighteenth? A twenty-first?

Lola leant back on the bench and thought about the last few weeks. She wasn't where she thought she was going to be, and she wasn't doing what she thought she'd be doing. But she found she didn't mind that. Maybe she hadn't found her mother, but she had found something else — something that was almost impossible to name.

Sam sat down beside her and handed her an ice-cream cone.

'Chocolate mint and double choc-chip,' he said.

Lola gasped. 'This is just what I felt like, ice-cream.'

'Chocolate ice-cream.' He gave her a look that made her laugh.

'Yes, chocolate ice-cream.' She took a lick and made a face of joy. She kept licking and slurping while Sam watched her, amusement playing across his face.

'You are the most enthusiastic eater I have ever known.'

Lola ignored him as she focused on her ice-cream.

Sam ate his slowly while Lola almost inhaled hers, but she didn't care. Sitting with Sam beside the river, in the warm night air, she felt more at home than she could remember. She tried to figure out why this was but couldn't. Was it because of nearly-but-not losing her dad? Because of seeing Babcia so happy with Clyde? Because she was here with Sam? She turned to Sam, catching him looking at her with a funny expression on his face.

'Mmm?'

'I'm just taking a mental snapshot of us,' he said, and looked ahead again.

'What for?'

'So when I need to remember contentment, what it looks like, I can recall this moment. It's better than feeling happy. It's serenity in action. This is feeling content. I'd forgotten what it felt like.'

Lola felt tears prick her eyes. She reached out and took his hand and they sat on the bench, sticky hand in sticky hand, eating ice-cream, a picture of serenity in action.

'You're wearing a red ribbon,' said Lola as she looked down at his hand in hers. The ribbon stood out next to his worn leather bracelets.

'Babcia put it on me.'

Lola laughed. 'You know, you're very lucky to have that.'

'I'm lucky for lots of reasons,' he replied.

Lola couldn't think of anywhere else in the world she would rather be.

19

Three nights later, Sam was nervously waiting for the cafe's first dinner service to start. Opening time was twenty minutes away and, even though he was as prepared as he could be, he still knew that surprises were probably in store. That was how restaurant life worked. *You don't always get what you ordered*, he reminded himself as he checked his list for the umpteenth time.

Sam and Lola had talked about food for three days straight, not mentioning the hand-holding or the admission that there was a two-way crush going on. But it seemed the more they tried to ignore it, the more the attraction grew between them.

Lola had stood just a little closer than necessary when they worked at the bench. Or was that his imagination running away?

Sam felt a jolt every time his hand or arm brushed hers when he reached for something near her.

They had decided to offer only a few beautifully done dishes. Lola was his sous-chef, as agreed. The starters were Mexican: soft-shell crab tacos or vegetarian nachos with the best guacamole Sam had ever tasted, courtesy of Lola's recipe.

'See, you can do more than just bake,' he'd said, taking another taste of the delicious lime-spiked mashed avocado.

'I know, but baking's so much prettier,' she'd replied.

The second course was a choice between a perfect duck pappardelle and a spring vegetable risotto. And for dessert, Lola had invented a frozen chocolate pudding with a fondant centre, served on an ice-cream stick. There'd also be a classic pavlova with a selection of toppings for the customers to create their own perfect desserts.

'They'll get little bowls of crumbled peppermint crisp, summer berries, passionfruit pulp, little chocolate chips – milk, white and dark – and then, finally, salted toffee shards.'

'That's insane,' Sam had laughed at the time.

But now that Lola had done it, and all the little meringue nests were lined up, ready to be served and self-decorated, Sam was happy to acknowledge the genius in the idea.

Kelsey, Fiona and Rosie were all waitressing, and Sanjay and his cousin were on dishes.

Now all they needed were customers.

Lola hadn't wanted to take bookings. She just said she would tell the regulars and see what happened. Even though Sam was sceptical, he didn't want to argue with her about it – not when she had put so much work into everything.

She was as gung-ho as ever, and Sam did everything she asked of him in the cafe. But the more she acted as though nothing had happened, nothing had changed between them, the more he wanted her.

It had never been like that with Katherine. No, Lola was a completely different person. There were no similarities between the two, except that he thought about them both all the time. But that wasn't quite true. Lately it had been Lola on his mind – even more than Katherine. He couldn't decide whether or not he should feel guilty about that.

He hadn't rung Katherine's phone in ages. He didn't have time, or when he did he was with Lola. She was probably his best friend. And she was his boss. That was why it was all so complicated. Sam's thoughts were interrupted by the familiar sound of the bell on the front door ringing, and he cleared his head.

Lola poked her head out through the servery window and looked into the cafe. She turned back to Sam and smiled. 'We're in business.'

And then they were off. Before long they had all tables filled and Sam was barking orders at Lola, moving at light speed as he worked.

Four hours later it was all over. Sam, sweaty, tired and over-come with emotion, walked outside to the small courtyard.

'I made it,' he said to the night sky.

'You did.'

He turned to see Lola behind him, the light from the cafe outlining her in her white T-shirt and black leggings. She walked towards him and looked up at the sky as well.

'He did it, and he was bloody amazing,' she called out into the night air, head thrown back.

Sam chuckled. 'Who are you talking to?'

'Katherine,' she shrugged. 'I assume you were telling her you made it through, and I wanted to confirm that you were great.'

Sam watched her face as she spoke, half-lit, tired, but so pretty.

'You don't think I'm mad?'

'Nope, whatever floats your boat, dude,' she laughed. 'I'm the last one to talk about coping mechanisms when you lose the most important person in your life.'

Sam sighed. 'I didn't know if I could do it, you know. Cook again like that,' he said quietly. 'After she died, everything seemed so hard, the idea of returning to my old life without her in it seemed . . . well, impossible.'

Lola nodded, silent.

'I'd forgotten how much I love food, and this world,' he gestured back towards the kitchen. 'I adore it, everything about it, and you allowed me to see that again, Lola. I can't thank you enough.'

Sam wanted to say more but he was getting all mushy and emotional. What Lola had given him was more than just food. It was friendship. He was changed because of her, and for the better.

Lola reached out and squeezed his hand, then turned and walked inside. Sam looked back at the sky. *Give me a sign, Katherine*, he silently said to the sky. *I love you, and always will. But I think I'm falling for Lola. What the hell am I going to do?*

He heard Fiona calling his name and walked back towards the kitchen, where he could see all the staff were standing around, drinks in hand.

'To Sam.'

They all cheered as he walked through the door. Sam felt himself laugh, and then the tears came. He stood there, feeling like a massive idiot, crying and laughing as Lola stepped forward and handed him an ice-cold beer.

'Thank you,' she whispered in his ear as she hugged him.

He held her for a long time, his face buried in her hair. And Sam knew what he needed to do to repay Lola for rebuilding him. He would find her mother for her. He would help her find the peace that she had given him.

20

Lola slowly climbed the stairs after they finished for the night. She was exhausted. Every bit of her ached. Checking her watch, she saw that in a few hours she had to be up again. But it had been worth it. They had made great money tonight — she'd finally be able to pay the overdue water bill — and it had been fun.

Sam was sitting on the sofa, still in his work clothes, a book in his hands.

'How good was tonight?' she said, falling onto the sofa next to him.

Sam gave her a funny little smile. 'Um, Lola?' he began, slowly, like he was going to say something serious. Lola felt her heart skip a beat. 'I found something,' he went on. 'I promise I wasn't snooping, but I came across this and I think it might be what you were talking about the other night. The note you mentioned that was found in your pram?'

He handed her a slip of paper from inside the old book he was holding. Lola took the note in two hands, like it might be snatched away at any moment. The handwriting was unfamiliar.

She read aloud. 'I can't help another person live their life until I have lived some of mine first. Clyde will tell you where to get hold of me once I settle in London. Sorry. Viv.' She felt a flash of rage. 'What a selfish bitch,' she cried, crumpling up the note and throwing it at the wall.

Sam said nothing as Lola stood up and paced the room.

'She can't help me live my life?' Lola spat out the words. 'I was a baby, for god's sake! Her baby! What sort of bullshit is that?'

Sam shook his head, speechless.

'No wonder Dad never mentioned it. No wonder Clyde said he couldn't remember what it said. This note shows what a cow my mother really is.' Lola was crying, ranting. 'She went to London to be an actress! What a fucking joke,' she screamed as Sam pulled her to him. 'What a joke,' Lola sobbed over and over into his chest. 'What a joke.'

Finally, after she'd calmed down a bit, she looked up at Sam and did what she had wanted to do for a long time: she kissed him. His lips were warm and firm, perfect.

'No, Lola,' Sam pulled away. 'You're upset. Not now. Not like this.'

'Like what?' she said, angry all over again. 'You've been looking at me for weeks like you want to kiss me – and now you don't?'

'Yes, I want to kiss you,' he said, his voice husky. 'But not like this, not when you're doing it to stop feeling bad about your mother.'

'Oh, piss off,' Lola yelled, hardly able to see for fury. How many rejections was she expected to stomach? She marched into her room, slamming the door behind her.

She had felt sorry for her mum when Clyde told her she wasn't coping with being a mum, but that note just made her so angry. If she didn't want a baby then she shouldn't have got pregnant.

Screw her, thought Lola. *I don't even want to find her anymore.* If her mother had wanted to know Lola, then she could have easily found her. The woman was a selfish bitch who didn't deserve her as a daughter.

She somehow managed to fall asleep in the early hours of the morning despite all the emotions whirling within her. Good thing the cafe opened a little later on a Sunday. But she was woken only a few hours later by the sound of Babcia's voice coming up the stairs.

'Looooola!'

'Oh god,' said Lola, coming out of her bedroom and seeing Sam in the hallway. 'Get your stuff and get into my room,' she hissed.

He looked at her, confused.

'Babcia is here!'

'It's five-thirty in the morning.' Sam rubbed his eyes and yawned.

'I know, and she will have been up since four-thirty, so move it.'

Sam shoved his pack under the bed and grabbed everything else in his arms, tiptoeing across the hallway into Lola's room.

Lola was at the top of the stairs trying to buy some time. 'Babcia,' she called, 'I'm just getting dressed. I'll be down soon. Wait for me in the kitchen.'

'Vhy?' said Babcia, climbing the stairs resolutely. She sat down heavily on the top step. 'I can vait here.'

'Relax downstairs, Babcia, and I'll get you a coffee.'

'No. I come to speak to you about somethink important,' she said firmly.

'I have to get ready for work.' Lola tried to think of a way to get Babcia back downstairs, but Babcia stood up and moved over to the sofa. Lola knew from experience it would probably take a while to budge her grandmother.

'Get dressed. Then ve talk.'

Lola knew she had lost this round — but then again, she pretty much always lost with Babcia. She went into her bedroom and saw Sam sitting at her desk, looking at the photos pinned to the wall.

'She's not going to go,' whispered Lola. 'Don't turn around. I have to get dressed.'

She shimmied into underwear and then pulled on some pink shorts and a rainbow-coloured halter neck top.

'Okay, I'm decent.'

Sam turned around. 'So what do we do?' he asked.

Lola brushed her hair and pulled it into a topknot. 'I have no idea.'

'You could just tell her the truth. We don't have anything to hide, really.'

'You don't know my Babcia,' said Lola, one eyebrow raised.

'Loooola?' she heard from the living room.

Lola pretended to slam her head against the closed door.

'I could escape through the window, like Spiderman.'

Lola nodded. 'Yep. Let's do it.'

'I was joking.'

'I'm not.' Lola rushed to the window and looked out.

'No, I'm not bloody doing it,' said Sam crossly, as Lola opened the old sash window and pulled off the flywire.

She put her head and upper body out the window. 'It's not that far. Hold my legs.'

'Why are you the one escaping?' asked Sam as he held on to Lola's legs.

'Good point, I'm panicking. Pull me back.'

She felt Sam's hand on her thighs and then on her hips as she fell back into the room and into Sam's arms.

She looked up at him, adrenaline coursing through her body as she tried to catch her breath. Sam's hands were still on her hips, and she felt him tighten his grip as he pulled her to him.

'Now?' she gasped, but she couldn't pull herself away.

'Lola?' she heard Babcia call, closer this time.

Lola jumped away from Sam as the bedroom door opened. Babcia stood in the doorway.

'Good morning, Sam,' Babcia said calmly. 'Can you let go of

Lola for a minute vhile I talk to her?'

Sam nodded, mute. Lola gave him a panicked look as she followed her grandmother out into the living room.

'It's not what it looks like, Babcia. Sam's –'

'I know about you young girls, I've vatched *Sex and the City*,' Babcia said airily. 'You like to try before you marry these days.'

'Marry? God, Babcia, I don't think so,' Lola said, but she felt relief wash over her.

'You never know,' said Babcia sagely.

Lola looked at the crumpled note on the floor, left there since last night. She reached down and picked it up, smoothing it out on her leg.

'Did you know about this?' she asked and handed it to Babcia, who took her glasses out of her bag and read it slowly.

'Yes, I knew.'

'Is that why you were so angry with Clyde?'

'I thought Clyde knew vhere she vas, and vouldn't tell us. But now I know he didn't know. No-one knew.' Babcia shrugged, but Lola could see the pain and regret on her face. 'I blamed him for a long time and I was wrong.'

Lola smiled a little. 'I'm glad you're friends again now.'

'He is coming to the Polish Club with me tomorrow night to play cards,' said Babcia proudly. 'It is nice to have somethink to look forward to, isn't it?'

Lola smiled, her eyes filling with tears. 'Yes, it is, Babcia,' she said, reaching out and taking her grandmother's hands. 'Now, why did you come to talk to me so early on a Sunday morning?'

Babcia took a deep breath and then looked at Lola, her face so serious that Lola felt nervous.

'Who is that voman who is visiting David? The vun vith the terrible clothes?'

Lola laughed. 'That's Jane, the bookkeeper. She's very nice, Babcia, so don't scare her off.'

Babcia pursed her lips disapprovingly. 'Yesterday I saw them kiss in the garden at the hospital.'

Lola felt her jaw drop open. 'No way.'

'Yes vay.'

∼

Lola watched Sam working in the kitchen later that day. It seemed that everyone in the city was getting some — everyone except her.

Sam moved fluidly around the space, completely in charge, all his senses on alert. Lola thought he had never looked sexier or more confident. Not in the cocky way of someone like that idiot, Andrew, but in a way that showed he was the boss of his domain and in complete control.

Is that what Mum saw in Dad? she wondered as Sam looked up at her, catching her staring.

'What?' he asked, his face tensing.

'I just wanted to say I'm sorry about last night,' she said. 'All of it.'

164

'That's okay,' he said lightly, and he turned his back to her and continued with his work.

But she wasn't sorry she kissed him. She was only sorry he didn't kiss her back.

21

Lola bit into the strawberry that Sam held out for her.

'Delicious, isn't it? You can taste the sunshine.'

'Wanker,' said Lola, laughing.

It was later the following week and Lola was helping Sam prep for dinner service. 'You seriously have to meet my dad,' said Lola, separating eggs. 'You two will have a big ol' food bromance.'

'How is he?' asked Sam. Lola hadn't said much about her dad recently.

'He's nuts,' said Lola, shaking her head. 'He's spouting advice about how to live your life to the fullest. He's talking about getting his ear pierced, which is so lame I can't even begin to think about it. And he thinks he wants to open a real restaurant. And Jane's, like, super keen on all this. I thought she'd be a stabilising influence, but she's encouraging him.' Lola made a face.

'What's the face for? Don't you like her?' Sam had spotted Jane talking to Lola a few times in the cafe, but he hadn't met her yet.

'Oh, I like her a lot, but Dad's a head-case. I don't know if he'll always be like this. It might just be a post-accident thing. I'd hate to see Jane get hurt. She's so nice and she's been so helpful.'

Lola went into the coolroom and came out carrying a large bunch of parsley.

Sam frowned as he worked. It had been nearly a week since he had started looking for Lola's mother and he'd come up with nothing, even with Clyde helping him.

Plus, he was borrowing Lola's laptop to do his detective work, which meant he was forever snapping it shut when she walked past, and having to remember to clear the history. Sam had zero experience being deceitful and he felt bad when Lola had looked at him in an odd way, asking a few times if he was okay. Sam had said something about trying to decide where to travel to next after her dad was back on his feet.

But the more Sam heard about Vivian and her life with David and little baby Lola, the more Sam understood how it might have gone wrong. He had seen it with his older sister when she had her first baby. The crying and the exhaustion. The sense of hopelessness. Eventually his mum had intervened, and taken her to the doctor. *Post-natal depression*, his mum had said, and everyone had to pitch in and help until his sister was all right again.

Sam didn't know whether it made it better or worse that Vivian had probably had post-natal depression. It still didn't explain where she was now. Why hadn't she come back? Even if she didn't want to be with David, she still had a child. Surely she'd want to see Lola.

These questions plagued him, and he found himself thinking about how much Lola had missed out on, growing up without a mum. But then, maybe she didn't think she had missed anything, given she'd never had it in the first place.

'What are you thinking about?' asked Lola, and Sam realised he'd been lost in thought, standing by the sink rinsing his already-clean knife.

'Oh, sorry, I was thinking about home.'

'Are you homesick?' She came to stand next to him at the sink.

'Not really,' said Sam honestly, as Sanjay walked in and hung his bag on the hook.

Sam and Lola smiled at Sanjay. The dinner crew was all there now, and just then Sam heard the bell of the cafe door chime, plunging him into work mode. All feelings for Lola and everything else in his head just shut down while he focused on the task in front of him.

It was about half an hour later when Fiona came skidding into the kitchen. 'That reviewer's here,' she said breathlessly, looking around the kitchen for a reaction.

Sam shrugged but Lola jumped on Fiona. 'From *The Weekly*?'

'Yes,' Fiona grabbed Lola's arm. 'Do you want me to throw

him out? Spill a drink on him? Tip beetroot juice on his shirt?'

'Why the hell would you want to do that to a reviewer?' asked Sam.

'Because he gave the Blueberry Cafe a great review because he's friends with the guy who runs it. Lola found out on her date with the owner, remember?' Fiona said, assuming Sam had been privy to the same goss she had. 'So he'll probably give us a bad review no matter what we do.' Fiona was almost purple with excitement and conspiracy theories.

'Is that true, Lola?' Sam asked. Lola hadn't said anything about a date with the owner of the competition. He hated the idea of Lola out on a date with anyone, and wasn't sure if this made it better or worse. He took a deep breath and reminded himself he had no claim on her.

'Yeah, but I'm not sure about this guy giving us a bad review.' Lola smiled to herself, and Sam wondered if he was about to hear about her great date or something. He turned back to the ducks he'd just pulled out of the oven.

'The owner was such a massive idiot,' giggled Lola to Fiona, within earshot of Sam. 'He was so full of himself.'

'I can't believe you poured your drink on him!' Fiona roared with laugher, recalling the story.

'Okay, so we cook for him as we would any customer,' Sam said firmly, but he couldn't resist a smile at Lola's story. 'We do our best and whatever the consequences, so be it.' He pushed Fiona out onto the cafe floor again. Lola spied through the servery window.

'He's with a woman. She looks weird.'

Sam ignored her as more orders came in. He got working again. 'Lola, move it. Now,' he barked.

Lola spun to look at him. 'You don't need to be rude,' she snapped as she moved into her position at the bench.

'My kitchen, my rules,' he said as he pushed the docket with an order for two serves of tacos along the bench towards her.

'My cafe, my rules,' she said sharply, picking up the order.

Sam ignored her. And Lola ignored him as she got to work, but he could hear her mumbling under her breath as she assembled the entrees. Sam saw Sanjay glance at them both, but he remained quiet. *Wise man*, thought Sam.

As the orders kept rolling in, Sam and Lola worked in silence, speaking only when it was totally necessary. Fiona and Kelsey moved in and out with the plates and kept a running commentary on the vibe of the reviewer and his guest.

'He seems okay, not overly nice but not a complete arse,' Fiona declared after clearing the dishes for the reviewer's dessert. Sam and Lola said nothing and Fiona quickly fled the kitchen.

'I think it's important that we just relax and do what we'd do for any customer,' Sam said evenly.

Lola nodded. 'I know. You're right. I just don't like taking orders from people.'

Sam looked at Lola's flushed face and laughed. 'You have to know by now I am the least bossy person in the world. Outside of the kitchen.'

Lola shrugged. 'I know.'

Fiona skidded into the kitchen. 'He's gone.'

'Did he say anything?' asked Lola.

'Nothing,' Fiona said. 'He just paid and left.'

'Well, that's it then,' sighed Lola, tears filling her eyes as she looked at Sam. 'One bad review and we're stuffed, like a turkey. All this for nothing.' She threw a tea towel onto the bench and headed into the coolroom, slamming the door shut behind her.

Sam glared at Fiona who quickly scuttled out of the kitchen again.

Sam opened the door to see Lola sitting on an empty milk crate.

'What?' she snapped, not looking at him.

Sam sat down next to her and took her hands in his. 'Why do you care so much what some reviewer thinks, when your whole thing is not caring what others think? That's what's so great about you.'

Lola looked up at Sam, tears streaming down her cheeks.

'I don't care what people think about me but I do care about what people think of the cafe. That's not just me. It's Dad. It's the business. And it's you.'

Sam held her hands up to his mouth and kissed them lightly. 'You are the sweetest, loveliest girl in the world. But you don't have to worry about what people think of me. I'm fine.'

Lola blinked at him. 'I know, but I don't want you to be fine. And I don't want you to be sad anymore either. I want you to be proud and happy about what you've achieved here.'

'I am.'

'I want you to be proud of the food.'

'I am.'

'I want you to be proud of me,' Lola said. Her face was so close to his, he could see the cute smattering of freckles across her nose, her long eyelashes and full lips.

'I am proud of you,' he murmured.

And then he kissed her. It was sweet and warm and every bit as good as he'd imagined, lying in bed at night. He groaned as he pulled her onto his lap. She felt incredible. They ran their hands through each other's hair feverishly as they kissed. Sam felt hot despite the temperature in the coolroom — and, from the way Lola was moving on his lap, she obviously felt the same.

'Lola?'

They heard a knock at the coolroom door and sprang to their feet. Kelsey put her head through, clearing her throat. 'We have two last dessert orders.'

Sam nodded professionally as he walked out into the kitchen, hoping his apron would hide his reaction to kissing Lola. He glanced awkwardly at Sanjay. Lola came out soon after, while Kelsey went back into the cafe.

Sam assembled the pavlova nests while Lola set up the accoutrements for the toppings. They said nothing, but Sam could see the blush of her cheeks whenever she looked at him. It was almost impossible not to reach out and touch her. He just wanted to pull her towards him and wrap his arms around her.

Sam didn't know when he had fallen for Lola but, as he finished the desserts with Lola beside him at the bench, he was pretty sure it was love. Even though it was different to what he'd had with Katherine, the intensity of his feelings was the same. It was actually funny how totally different Lola was to Katherine. Loud, impulsive, passionate and so sexy it was doing his head in.

He felt bad to be comparing the two. And it was surely insane to be thinking about love after one stolen kiss in the coolroom. He needed to get a grip.

Lola glanced at him, smiling as she headed out to the front of the cafe to debrief with the others.

When the last customers had left and Sanjay was nearly done with the dishes, Sam poured himself a glass of wine from the open bottle Fiona had brought to the kitchen and sipped it slowly. He was now half-wondering if he imagined the kiss in the coolroom. Did Lola regret it? Was she going to pretend it hadn't happened? Sam felt his stomach clenching with anxiety and desire.

The others were sitting at the big table out the front, and Sam took his wine and joined them. He sat next to Lola, not saying much.

He was just wondering what was going through Lola's head when he felt her hand on his leg under the table. She was tracing her fingernail gently up and down the inside of his thigh in a slow circular pattern. He reached down and grabbed her hand under the table, squeezing it. She circled his palm with her thumb. Sam thought he might explode from desire.

About twenty minutes later, although it felt longer than that to Sam, Lola pulled her hand away from Sam's and stood up. 'All right, go home the lot of you. Day off tomorrow.'

Fiona and Kelsey stared at her in shock.

'You've worked day and night for weeks, you are amazing and I want to say thank you.'

'What about the customers? What if they go to Blueberry?' asked Kelsey.

'Honestly, even if they get their coffee from Blueberry tomorrow, I have no doubt they will be back,' Lola said cheekily, as she opened the front door and ushered everyone out. 'Go on, off into the night with the lot of you. I'll finish the pack up tomorrow. I'm shattered.'

Sam sat watching as Kelsey, Sanjay and Fiona grabbed their things, kissed Lola and waved Sam goodbye. He stood up in the empty cafe, nearly empty wine glass in hand, as Lola shut the door and locked it behind the others.

'Do I get the day off too?' he asked, surprised by how nervous he felt.

Lola walked up to him and took the glass from his hand. She took a sip and put it down on the table.

'No, you don't get the day off,' she said, taking his hands and pulling him to her, kissing him passionately.

A loud banging on the glass of the cafe window startled them both and they jumped apart, guilty. In the light of the street lamp they could see Kelsey, Fiona and Sanjay all whooping and cheering at them through the window. Lola stuck her middle finger up at them good-naturedly and Sam grabbed Lola and kissed her again, just to make sure the moment was real.

22

Lola could feel Sam, hard against her as they kissed outside her bedroom door. She moved towards her door but felt Sam hesitate.

'We don't have to do anything, you know,' she said. Lola held his hands tight and kissed him again. 'One day at a time.' She opened her bedroom door and playfully pushed Sam towards his own room. She figured it was all too much, too soon. Katherine and all that. But this time she didn't feel the sting of rejection.

Sam stood in the hallway for a moment, looking at her, clearly as turned on as she was. But still holding himself back, resisting.

Then he moved so swiftly, he nearly knocked her off her feet. He was kissing her and pulling her hair from the bun at the nape of her neck. His hands were in her hair and around her hips and everywhere at once. Lola pulled him onto the bed, where they fell, Sam half on top of her.

Lola pulled at his jeans and Sam tried to take Lola's T-shirt off at the same time, and they smashed their heads together.

'Owww,' they said in unison, laughing.

'I'm seriously out of practice,' said Sam, making a face to hide his embarrassment.

Lola lay next to him and giggled. 'We're perfectly choreographed in the kitchen but have no idea in the bedroom.'

Sam looked at her with the half-smile that Lola was growing to adore.

'Come on, then,' he said and climbed off her and pulled her up off the bed.

'Huh?' said Lola as he led her into the hallway and down the stairs, holding her hand all the while.

In the dark kitchen, lit only by the light from the street lamps coming in from the front, Lola stood, her eyes gradually adjusting.

Sam was behind her, close, his hands on her waist.

'When I cook and you are near me,' he whispered in her ear, 'it takes everything I have to not pull you close and kiss you.'

His voice was husky with desire and Lola felt herself lean back into him. As she turned, their lips met. And then it was on.

Hands, mouths, clothes off, no words, no head banging or laughing. It was the most intense experience that Lola had ever had with a guy.

Sam was in charge in the kitchen and he was in charge now.

As he lifted Lola onto the bench she wrapped her legs around him. She looked at him, the light catching his face, and thought how gorgeous he was. He was probably her best friend, and she wondered if this was the right thing to be doing.

Once, she wouldn't have thought twice about it, but she'd changed — things were different now. She wriggled away and closed her legs, feeling vulnerable on the bench in the nude.

'I don't think we should do this,' she murmured, taking his hand away from her breast.

'Really?' asked Sam. 'I thought we just were.'

'I don't want to ruin our friendship.'

'We won't,' he said softly, planting little kisses along her shoulder.

'I don't want you to leave because things get weird.'

'I won't,' he replied, the kisses heading down towards her nipple.

Lola took a deep breath and gently pushed him away so she could look at him properly. He was incredibly sexy in the nude.

'I want you, seriously I do. But I still think we're both really messed up.'

'We're naked in a commercial kitchen. I cannot imagine the health and safety codes we're violating right now,' Sam admitted.

Lola got off the bench and picked up her clothes.

'We need to talk,' she said and ran up the stairs, hoping her bottom wasn't wobbling too much in front of Sam.

Lola ran to her bed and jumped in and held the covers up for

Sam. He glanced down at her nakedness and rolled his eyes.

'You cannot expect me to lie naked next to this glorious body and not want to inhale every part of you.'

Lola giggled as Sam got into bed beside her. He lay on his side, an arm under his head.

'Lola.'

'Yes.'

They stared at each other.

'You don't really know what you want, do you?'

'I have no freakin' idea,' she admitted. 'About anything.'

'Not even me?'

'You?' she sighed, thinking. 'You I want to love and adore and kiss every day for the rest of my life.'

'And the problem with that is?'

'You work for me, you have green eyes — which are known to be bad luck — you're a backpacker from the other side of the world, and you have a dead fiancée who you still occasionally talk to on the phone.'

Sam laughed until tears poured down his cheeks.

'All right, I'll see your list and raise you. Well, first, you're my boss, next, you have red hair — which everyone knows is a sign of an angry person — you're an okay cook but you lack focus, and you have a missing mother whose abandonment has coloured everything in your life so far. You also have a crazy father who has suddenly found his verve for life and a grandmother who winds red ribbons around the wrists of everyone she likes.'

'God, we're a pair of head cases,' Lola groaned. Everything Sam said was true but she wasn't mad at him for pointing it out. She felt nothing but love towards him. She moved closer.

'You know you're my best friend now,' she whispered.

'And you're mine.'

He kissed her nose and her forehead and then each cheek and finally her mouth. The passion and lust in the kitchen was replaced with tenderness as they moved in perfect rhythm. It was slow and careful, Lola gasping as she felt him inside her. He kissed her neck and then pinned her hands above her head.

There was something about the way they moved together that was different from sex with other boys. Sam was more present, more focused on making sure Lola was ready, comfortable, taken care of. Lola felt more desired than she ever had before, and she felt sexy — that was the main difference. Not like a girl, but like a woman.

When they lay together afterwards, their hands intertwined, Lola's head on his chest, she knew that this wasn't just sex with some backpacker.

'Sam?' she said quietly.

'Lola.' His voice came from deep inside his chest.

'Would it be weird if I said I might fall in love with you if I stayed here?'

'So, stay,' he said simply, and he rolled over to look at her.

'I can't,' she said. 'I have to find my mother. I need to sort it out in my head. Finish it, you know?'

She felt him playing with her hair.

'Lola?'

'Sam.' She smiled as she said his name.

'I'd like you to stay. But to ask you to do that would be wrong, kind of like holding you back. You have to do what's right for you.'

'I know,' she sighed.

'And eventually your dad will come back and I'll have to leave anyway.'

'I know,' said Lola, her voice catching in the dark.

'Are you okay?' he asked after a while.

Lola nodded and then moved so she could see his face.

'You?'

'I'm better than fine,' he said, and pulled her close and kissed her again.

Then she fell asleep, dreaming about chocolate mousse and long kisses with Sam. Then she was serving Clyde and Babcia in the cafe while Sam stood outside with his backpack on, waving goodbye, leaving her to run the cafe on her own with no water.

23

Lola was just bringing a classic toasted ham-and-cheddar sandwich out of the kitchen when a voice interrupted her.

'Morning,' she heard, and looked up to see Jane on the other side of the counter.

Today she was wearing a T-shirt with a sequined rainbow on it. It was actually not bad. Or was Lola just getting used to Jane's fashion?

'Have you seen it?' asked Jane, her face flushed with excitement.

'Seen what?'

'The review!' Jane waved *The Weekly* at Lola, who snatched it off her and shoved the sandwich at Fiona.

'Table eight,' Lola barked, as she flipped to the food section.

Cafe Ambrosia doesn't look like much, but this little gem of a place is better than anything in the area. The cafe's new dinner menu is thoughtfully created by British import Sam Button, clearly a rising star.

Everything about our evening was excellent, but an honourable mention goes to the desserts, made by Lola Batko, daughter of owner David Batko. I had a creative pavlova affair with DIY toppings, and my partner could have eaten two more of her frozen chocolate pudding on a stick. Both were exquisite and inventive — Batko junior is a talent to watch in the dessert world.

The young, pleasant waitstaff were attentive and energetic but treated me like any other customer.

I implore you to visit Cafe Ambrosia before Sam Button goes back to the UK or Lola Batko sets her horizons further afield. You won't regret it.

Lola ran into the kitchen and started jumping up and down, waving the paper at Sam.

'Read it, we're amazing!' she yelled.

Sam calmly wiped his hands on his apron and took the paper.

He read the review slowly while Lola nearly burst with frustration.

'Hurry up!'

'Shhh,' he waved his hand at her. 'I'm marinating in the words.' When he finally looked up, he was beaming with pride. 'How good is what they said about your desserts?'

'And you and your food,' said Lola, hugging him, dizzy with happiness.

'You need to keep making desserts. You love it, and you're amazing at it.' He picked up the paper and read the review again.

'We're amazing,' said Lola as she peered over his shoulder.

'This is my first review,' said Sam, turning to Lola. 'I have to scan it and send it to Mum. She's gonna flip. She'll be telling everyone she meets about it. They'll never hear the end of it, I swear.'

Lola smiled, but felt some of the fizz die down. She was happy for Sam, really. But there was no mother for her to share her news with. And then she recovered a little. No point being a sad sack about it.

'I'm going to check if Jane has shown Dad yet,' she said, heading back into the cafe where Jane was drinking coffee and talking to Clyde, who had become quite the regular.

'I didn't know you two knew each other,' said Lola as she walked over to the pair.

'We met at the rehab centre,' laughed Jane.

'Oh,' said Lola, feeling a bit odd about that.

'We sometimes all have lunch in the cafeteria. It's not as good as here, but their soup isn't bad,' said Clyde, turning to Jane.

Lola swallowed, knowing she was being petty. But why hadn't they asked her? Here she was, working so hard, day after day, while they all met for lunches. Even if she did love the cafe, she still resented that no-one had bothered to ask her.

Jane was watching Lola's face. 'It just happened,' she explained. 'It wasn't planned or anything. Clyde's been driving Gisella to the rehab centre, and to be honest, it's nice to have Clyde around. To, you know, deflect Gisella's opinions.'

Lola nodded and walked back into the kitchen.

'Do you ever feel like everyone has a life, but you?' she asked Sam, watching as he expertly tossed some mushrooms in a pan.

'Constantly,' he said and Lola laughed.

'I want to go out and dance on tables, but now this review's out, we'll be busier than ever.' She sighed. 'Being a grown-up sucks,' she declared, heading upstairs to take a break.

Lola lay on the sofa and stared at the ceiling. She knew she didn't have time to have a meltdown in the middle of service, but she just needed a few minutes.

'Lola?' she heard, Jane's face appearing at the top of the stairs.

'Hi,' said Lola, waving at Jane but staying slumped on the couch.

'I think we've made you upset,' said Jane, sitting down on the chair opposite her.

'No, it's fine. I'm just tired and oversensitive, that's all.'

'I can see why you'd feel hurt,' said Jane. 'But honestly, it was just a few times and we didn't plan it. I won't lie – your grandma is hard work.'

Lola sat up. 'I know, I know.'

'It's lucky I'm older. I don't think I would have coped with her if I was younger and more sensitive.'

'Like my mother,' said Lola, the thought occurring to her for the first time. 'I don't think Babcia would have made life very easy for her.'

'Sorry?'

'You know my mother left when I was a baby?'

Jane nodded. 'You mentioned it when we first met.'

'She went out for a walk one day and then just got on a bus, leaving me by the letter box in my pram.'

'Wow.'

'So I guess that's why I have issues about being left behind,' laughed Lola grimly. 'I probably need to see a shrink.' She tapped her head with her knuckles for effect.

'I think you've turned out pretty great,' said Jane softly.

There was a silence. 'You like him a lot, don't you?' Lola finally asked, although she already knew the answer.

Jane blushed. 'I do. I've liked him ever since I discovered the cafe, but I was too shy to talk to him. You did me a favour, sending me to see him.' She giggled like a teenager and Lola rolled her eyes.

'You young kids,' she mocked.

Jane stood up and so did Lola. 'Your review was amazing,' said Jane, giving Lola a hug. 'I'm proud of you.'

Jane smelled of fresh laundry and flowers. Lola relaxed into her.

'Thanks,' she said as she pulled away and looked at Jane's T-shirt. 'I have to ask you, where do you get your clothes from?'

Jane laughed. 'My mother lives in Queensland and owns a fashion boutique. She sends them to me. I used to hate them but now I'm kind of used to them, and people know me for my crazy tops. Also, I'm really shy and my tops are a great conversation starter.'

Lola smiled. 'That's great. You're great. I'm glad you and Dad are hanging out,' she said, meaning every word.

'If you're very lucky I might get Mum to send you one.' Jane headed back down the stairs.

'Promises, promises,' called Lola, laughing.

24

Sam put down the phone in shock. It was so simple, and yet so utterly devastating.

Lola's mother had never even made it to England. She'd died in Western Australia, soon after leaving Melbourne. She'd been staying with her parents at the time – parents who had only now found out they had a granddaughter.

Sam had run out of leads in his search for Vivian in England, and had instead focused his search in Australia. Lola only had a few details about her mother from the wedding certificate, including the lie that Vivian's parents were deceased. David had never questioned this, and so hadn't bothered to search for her family.

But there were so many inconsistencies in her story, even after all these years, that Sam could see which threads he needed to pull for it to fall apart.

How would a nineteen-year-old leave the country without a passport or money? How did someone just disappear off the face of the earth? Something had to have happened. Someone had to have helped her disappear.

Surprisingly, finding Vivian's relatives wasn't so hard. Sam knew Lola's mum was from Perth, so he started by ringing all the Sanderses listed in that region. He used his own phone, not caring about the bill. He just needed to get Lola some answers.

But now that he had those answers, he felt sick. When Katherine died, he had hated the world for being so unfair. But at least he knew what had happened and had been able to grieve.

Lola had her mind set on finding her mother. She was angry and hurt at being abandoned, but now she would have to turn all that anger and pain into grief instead.

Sam heard Lola clattering up the stairs. He fixed a bright smile to his face. He didn't want to tell her — not yet. Things were so great between them. Today was their one day off, and Lola was back from seeing her dad.

'What's cooking?' she asked.

'Nothing, thankfully,' he answered, as she settled in his lap. 'How's your dad?'

'Good. He's moving around with the frame now. They're saying he'll be home soon. But now that he's decided he's going to change his life, I'm afraid to ask what that means.'

Sam played with the little tendrils of hair escaping Lola's bun at the nape of her neck.

'What does he want to do with the cafe?'

'I don't know,' Lola sighed. 'I don't even know if I want to keep running it. But this whole thing has made me sure of one thing. I need to get my shit together and start to plan for the future.'

Sam kissed her. 'You'll work it out.'

Lola snuggled into his neck. 'I want Dad to be better, but I'm not sure I want to give up what we have going. I love being with you.'

He had been thinking the same thing. He had to go home eventually — his visa only had another eight months on it. But what would happen when he got home? Everyone would expect him to still be grieving for Katherine, and here he was, falling for a red-headed Aussie girl.

Lola's phone rang. She made a face at the screen. 'It's Babcia.'

'You should take her call.'

Lola and her grandma hadn't seen each other much in the past week or so, and Sam knew it bothered Lola more than she expressed. Lola nodded and took the call.

'Hi, Babcia. Okay, I know. I'm sorry too.' Lola stood up. 'Okay, yes. Okay. Bye.'

Lola turned to Sam. 'I have to go and see Babcia. She's being lonely and weird. I know it's our day off, but I have been a bit of a bitch lately.'

Sam nodded. 'Of course, go, go. I'll chill here and we'll see each other when you get back.'

Lola kissed his cheek. 'You know my family is crazy, right?'

'They all are,' he laughed as Lola grabbed her bag and headed downstairs.

After he heard the door slam, Sam went to the pile of bills on the desk in the corner. Finding what he needed, he grabbed his keys, grabbed some supplies from the kitchen and then left the cafe.

Sam waited for the bus, not entirely sure he was heading in the right direction, but knowing for sure what he had to do with the information he had.

Two buses later, Sam had arrived. He stood out the front of the building and took a deep breath before heading inside. After asking the woman at the desk which way to go, he headed down the corridor until he came to the right door. He knocked, and was invited in by a cheery voice.

Inside sat a man reading a book with the title, *Getting Unstuck – Live the Life You Deserve.*

'Hello,' Sam said, more than a little shyly.

'Hi,' said the man pleasantly. 'Can I help you?'

'I'm Sam. The guy who's cooking at Ambrosia?'

Lola's father smiled broadly and extended his hand towards Sam. 'David. Pleased to meet you. Lola says you're fantastic.'

'She's the one who's fantastic. She's done amazing things with the cafe.'

'I read the review,' said David. 'Your food is quite a hit.'

Sam smiled, but he still felt nervous, worried. He put a large shopping bag on the table. 'Some chicken salad, a few mangos and some of Lola's vanilla and raspberry panna cotta.'

David peeked inside the bag. Sam saw that Lola and her father shared the same beaming smile where food was concerned.

'Sit, sit,' David gestured to the chair beside the bed.

Sam did as he was told, clasping his hands in his lap.

David leant forward. 'I'm glad you've popped in. I was hoping we might talk.' He paused, and then whispered conspiratorially, 'Actually, I was hoping you might stay on.'

'At the cafe?' Sam shook his head slowly. 'Thank you for the offer, and believe me, it's tempting. But I've decided I need to finish my apprenticeship. I'm only a year away.'

David nodded, looking disappointed but understanding. 'How's my Lola coping?' he asked.

'She's great, she's amazing,' said Sam, wondering if his feelings for her would be obvious.

David nodded, approving of Sam's review. 'My mother tells me you two are great friends.'

Sam had a nasty feeling he was about to be interrogated.

'We are,' agreed Sam carefully.

'Lola had to put off her London trip because of my accident.'

'I know,' said Sam. Where was this going? What had Babcia said about them?

'She was going to find her mother. Did you know Lola's mother ran away when Lola was just a baby?'

Sam nodded.

David looked away at the trees outside the window. 'For nearly eighteen years I've waited for Viv to come back, torn between worry, anger and deep hurt.'

Sam was silent.

'I didn't deal with anything properly. Grief does that to you.' He turned back to Sam. 'And I can see the effect that's had on Lola. Perhaps I didn't try hard enough to find Viv. And not pursuing my own dreams hasn't made me much of a role model to Lola.'

Sam went to disagree, but David put up his hand.

'Don't wait for life to deliver what you want,' he said. 'You have to make things happen.' As he spoke, he had a gleam in his eye.

Sam smiled at him. 'Good advice.'

David laughed. 'But you didn't come here to take advice from a man with a broken pelvis and a walking frame. What can I do for you, Sam?'

'Actually, I wanted to talk to you about Lola's mother.'

'Her mother? Why?' David frowned.

God, this was a stupid idea, Sam thought. Death was the worst possible scenario. *But at least if you know, you have somewhere to start rebuilding from. It's not knowing that's holding Lola back.*

Kissing Katherine's cheek after they turned off the life support was the worst moment in his entire life. But at least it was an ending.

'Well?' prompted David, his good mood seeming to ebb away at the mention of his wife. It was obviously one thing for him to talk about Vivian, and quite another for Sam to.

'Um, it's just that Lola and I have become pretty close, and she mentioned some things to me,' Sam began nervously. 'I realised that she probably needs some closure on this, you know? Just to kind of get on with things and life and so on . . .' Sam's voice trailed off at the look on David's face.

There was a pause before David spoke. 'I appreciate your help with the cafe and I know you have provided great support to Lola. But I would prefer you focus on the professional and not the personal, if you don't mind.'

'Actually, I do mind,' said Sam with a sigh. *This was always going to be hard*, he reminded himself. But perhaps he hadn't fully realised how hard.

Before he could say any more, a woman walked into the room.

'Jane,' said David, clearly relieved at the interruption.

Jane smiled warmly at Sam. 'Hello!' she said, surprise in her voice. 'Is Lola here too?'

Sam stared at the sequined frogs on her T-shirt. 'No, she's with Babcia,' he said, feeling David glance at him.

Jane sat down on the extra chair and smiled at them both. 'This is nice, isn't it?' she said hopefully.

'Sam was just telling me all about Lola,' David said, an edge to his voice.

Sam looked at David. 'I found the notebook in the flat — the one with all your ideas? They were bloody brilliant.'

'Why the hell were you looking through my books?'

Sam decided to ignore the anger building in David's voice. 'In the book was the note that Vivian left in the pram,' said Sam, watching David's face carefully.

'You're out of line,' said David, trying to get up from his bed before slumping back into it, wincing.

'And you're in denial,' said Sam, shaking his head sadly. 'Lola needs to know what happened. It's eating her up.'

'Don't tell me about Lola, I raised her, for god's sake,' said David, his voice raised now.

Sam swallowed a few times, his mouth dry and his jaw tense. 'Vivian's dead,' he said in a low voice. 'I'm so sorry. I wanted to help Lola find her mother. But then I discovered Vivian died, all those years ago, not long after she left Melbourne.'

David's face was still, his mouth half-open, as though time had stopped.

It was Jane who leant forward, reaching a comforting arm to David. 'Are you sure, Sam?

Sam nodded.

'Where was she?' croaked David, his eyes filled with tears. 'How did she die? How did you find out?' His face was pale and his voice shook.

Jane jumped up to get him a glass of water from the jug by the bed.

David sipped the water absently and finally looked at Sam. 'I guess you'd better tell me everything you know.'

25

Sam walked up the street towards the cafe, his mind ticking over with what had happened with David. He thought again about how easy it had been, relatively speaking, to find out what had happened to Vivian. Had David just never really tried, or had part of him known all along that Vivian might have been dead? Perhaps he felt he was protecting them all by keeping them in the dark.

'Hey mate, you got a minute?' he heard as he passed the outdoor tables at Blueberry Cafe.

Sam stopped and turned to the man who was speaking to him — he was sitting outside, a sleek MacBook on the table in front of him.

'I'm Andrew, I'm a friend of Lola's,' the man explained. 'You got a minute?'

Sam frowned but sat down. He didn't want to be rude to a friend of Lola's.

'Lola told me what a great chef you are,' said Andrew. 'And people are raving about your food!'

Sam nodded politely as Andrew poured him some water from the jug on the table.

'Lola said you might be in the market for a new gig,' said Andrew. 'She said her dad was coming back, so they wouldn't need you anymore.'

'Really?'

'Yeah, so I was thinking, we're looking for a new chef here, someone with your talents.'

'This is your cafe?' asked Sam, now realising who this guy was. 'I appreciate the thought,' he said, standing up, 'but no thanks.' He extended his hand to Andrew who shook it with a smile.

'If you change your mind, let me know.'

'Will do,' said Sam, continuing towards Ambrosia.

No, his place was by Lola's side now. She was going to need him more than ever.

⁓

'You just took a job with Andrew, didn't you?' Lola said accusingly as he walked up the stairs a few minutes later. 'I saw you talking to him.'

'Huh?' Sam was shocked by the anger in Lola's face and voice.

'I saw you,' said Lola, her eyes narrowed. 'You were shaking his hand and acting all matey. You're a shitty person, Sam Button.' She strode into her father's bedroom and started to stuff Sam's belongings into his backpack.

'Lola, wait,' he said as he followed her into the room.

'Wait for what?' she snapped. 'Stay here so we can be in love,' she said in a mocking tone. 'Stay here so you can take a job with a prick of a guy who already tried to poach you from me.'

'Andrew offered me a job, yes,' Sam said. 'And I told —'

Lola interrupted him. 'Oh, Andrew, is it? First-name terms with the new boss.' She picked up a shoe and threw it at him.

'You're being crazy, Lola! Let me explain.'

'Explain what?' she said, still furiously shoving things into his backpack. 'It's inevitable. You'll leave me, just like my mum did. And now Dad with Jane. Even Babcia has Clyde. I am unlovable. That's why you're taking the job.'

'Lola, stop it!' he yelled, and Lola finally went quiet. 'Stop being so fucking melodramatic,' he said, pulling his backpack away from her. 'And let me explain. Yes, he offered me a job. And no, I didn't take it. I will be here as long as you want me to be.'

Lola stood still, her breath ragged.

'I am not your mother. And you're not really angry with Babcia and your dad for finally getting on with their lives. I know you're not. Your dad's accident shook things up, and secrets and lies have been uncovered. But I wouldn't betray you, or leave you. I love you.'

Lola stared at him for a long time, still speechless.

'I went and saw your dad today.'

'Okay, that's weird,' said Lola, frowning. 'Why?' She stood in front of him, hands on her hips, the backpack lying between them.

Sam hesitated.

'Tell me!'

'I found out what happened to your mum,' he said slowly.

Lola's eyes widened. 'And? Where is she?'

Sam led her to the bed and sat her on the edge of it.

'Why do you look like you're about to cry?' Lola asked, fear and suspicion lacing her voice.

'Because I might. Lola, you know I care about you, don't you?'

She nodded.

'You have done so much for me, healed me in so many ways, and I just wanted to do the same for you.'

'Okay,' said Lola, clearly impatient for him to get to the point. 'Is she in London? Did you talk to her?'

'Lola, your mum died.'

Lola burst into shocked tears. 'What? Are you sure? When?'

'Three months after she left you. She went back home to Perth, and was living with her parents again. She wasn't coping, Lola. She wasn't well.'

'What do you mean? She was sick?'

'Yes, she was sick.' Sam's eyes filled up with tears. He reached across and pulled Lola into a bear hug.

'I don't get it,' Lola was saying, clearly trying to put it all together. 'My mum had parents? I have other grandparents? Are they alive? Why didn't they tell us what happened?'

'Because they didn't know you existed. Your mum didn't tell them about you or your dad. They didn't even know she was married.'

Lola held on to Sam and sobbed. 'She didn't tell anyone about me? She hated me!'

'Shhh, no, she didn't. Lola, she was really unwell.'

'You keep saying that,' said Lola angrily as she pulled away from him. 'What was so wrong with her?'

'Lola . . . she took her own life.'

Lola gasped, her sobbing increasing again. Sam could only imagine that, of all the scenarios Lola had in her head, this was unlikely to be one of them. It was utterly devastating.

'Does my dad know?' Lola asked, wiping her tears away with the back of her hand and hunting around for a tissue.

'Yes.'

'You told him?'

Sam nodded.

'I have to go and see him,' said Lola, blowing her nose and standing up.

Sam nodded sadly, watching as Lola stood up and walked to the door. She turned at the doorway.

'Well?'

He looked at her, unsure what she meant.

'Are you coming or what?'

'I thought you'd want to go alone. I've made things hard enough already.'

Lola walked back into the room and took his hand. 'It's the most awful, loveliest thing anyone's ever done for me. I can't even imagine how shit it was for you to find this out and then have to tell me.'

Sam took her red and tear-streaked face in his hands. 'You know you're great, don't you? Even if you do jump to conclusions.'

'I know, maybe I am crazy. Like she was, obviously, if she killed herself.'

'Now don't you dare think that,' said Sam sternly. 'You are not your mother and you are not crazy. You need to talk to your grandparents and find out about her.'

'This is straight-up fucked,' sighed Lola.

'That's exactly what it is. Straight-up fucked.'

26

'I don't think I'm the most popular person with your dad,' Sam explained as they walked down the stairs and outside, heading to the bus stop.

'Of course you're not. But he'll learn to love you.' Lola took his hand.

Sam squeezed it tightly as they waited for a bus.

'You okay?' he asked her.

'I don't know. I have no idea what to feel. I feel like I should be sadder.'

Sam pulled her closer.

'I'm trying to figure out how you grieve for a mother you never knew.'

The bus pulled up and they got on. Lola stared out the window at the passing people in the twilight. She kept a tight hold of Sam's hand, not speaking, until they got to the hospital.

'You want to wait out here?' she asked as they walked down the corridor towards her father's room.

Sam nodded while Lola went inside.

David turned when Lola opened the door to his room. He'd been crying, and Lola felt her heart break at the sight of him. He looked exhausted.

'Oh, Dad,' she said, running to him and flinging her arms around him.

'I don't know why I'm so sad after all this time,' he sniffled.

'You loved her.'

'I did.'

There was a pause. 'I spoke to her parents after Sam left,' David said, releasing Lola from the hug. 'Your grandparents.'

Lola was silent.

'They're very sad. This has brought it all up again for them.'

Lola nodded.

'They didn't know about you,' David said, his voice quavering. 'She never told them. I know how much Babcia loves you, and it's so sad you didn't get another set of grandparents to love you.'

'It's okay, Dad.'

They held each other for a long time before Lola pulled away.

'Sam was good to help us, you know,' admitted David.

'I'm in love with him.' Lola didn't want any more secrets.

'And I think he's in love with you.'

Lola flushed with pleasure at that.

'And you do know that your mum loved you very much, don't you?' David said, his hands clasping hers.

'But I cried all the time,' she said in a quiet voice, wiping away her tears even as more fell.

'You mainly cried when you weren't with her.'

'Babcia said I cried so much that Mum couldn't cope.'

'You had colic. And all babies cry a lot. But honestly, Babcia was jealous that your mum was the only one who could soothe you.'

Lola looked down at her hands. 'So who soothed me after she left?' she asked.

David wiped a tear away from his cheek and squeezed Lola's hand. 'I did. And Babcia did. And you learnt to soothe yourself,' he said. 'It was as though you knew that she wasn't coming back and just got on with life.'

He paused for a moment, and then he gave her a little smile. 'You were the only one who did get on with your life. God knows I didn't.'

Lola glanced at the open doorway, through which she could see Jane and Sam talking quietly in the corridor.

'Don't wait any longer, Dad,' she said, turning back to him.

'For what?'

'For life to begin.'

David nodded and looked at the figures in the corridor. 'You too, Lollipop.'

27

Three weeks later, Lola stood outside an unfamiliar front door and exhaled slowly. She was grateful to have Sam hovering just behind her. Lola pressed the doorbell. There was the sound of footsteps, and then the door opened.

'Viola?' An older woman with white hair and red glasses stood holding the door open.

'Lola,' she replied, before she was swept up into a huge hug by the woman.

'Kevin, Lola's here,' the woman called over her shoulder.

The woman let Lola go and held her at arm's length, looking closely at her. 'Such a gorgeous girl, isn't she?' the woman said, turning for the first time to Sam.

'I think so.' Sam grinned.

'Come in, come in,' she said, ushering them inside and extending her hand to Sam. 'I'm Jan.'

Sam and Lola had flown over the day before. Kevin and Jan had insisted on paying for the tickets and Lola had closed the cafe for two days to meet her newly discovered grandparents.

Jan led them into the sitting room, where a frail man sat in an armchair. He didn't get up to greet her or Sam.

'Kevin,' said Jan slowly, 'this is Lola. Our granddaughter,' Jan's voice cracked with emotion as she spoke.

Kevin looked at Lola and nodded. She could see tears staining his lined cheeks.

'Kevin had a stroke a few years ago. It's hard for him to do much, but he knows exactly what's going on.'

Lola reached out and held the man's hand and then kissed his cheek. He grasped her hand tightly.

'I'm really pleased to be here,' she said, and looked up at Sam. 'This is my boyfriend, Sam. He's from London. He's a chef.'

Jan bustled off into the kitchen and soon reappeared with a tray of iced tea and fruit bun cut up neatly on a floral plate.

'Sit, sit,' she urged, putting the tray on the coffee table. 'We want to get to know you. Tell us a bit about yourself.'

Lola told Jan a few details, enough to make her sound happy and well adjusted but not so much that she didn't need a mother. After some more small talk, Lola cleared her throat.

'Do you have any pictures of my mother?' she asked tentatively.

'I only have a few.'

'Of course.' Jan stood up and walked into another room.

'You . . .'

Lola turned to see Kevin trying to say something. She moved closer and took his hand.

' . . . look like Vivi,' he finished.

Lola smiled and felt tears prick her eyes. On the way over in the hire car, Lola had thought she'd have to keep reminding herself that these people were her grandparents. But now she was there, the connection felt immediate.

Kevin paused again, and with great effort continued. 'You are her gift to us.'

Jan walked back into the room with three photo albums in her arms.

'Here we are,' she said, sitting down next to Lola and opening one of them.

Over the next three hours Lola learnt about her mother from birth to eighteen, when she'd abruptly left home. She learnt Vivian hated bananas like Lola, and, like Lola, loved dancing. She was creative, but didn't know what to do with her skills. She had done okay at school, but didn't know what to study. Just like Lola. But unlike Lola, she didn't have many friends; she was shy, anxious, and lacked confidence.

'Her illness started to show when she was at school,' Jan explained sadly. 'We got her some help, she was on medication for a while. But she hated taking the tablets. Then one day she just left home. All we had was a note saying she was going east.'

Lola listened as Jan spoke. Jan occasionally looked over to Kevin for reassurance, which he gave with his eyes.

'We didn't hear from her for nearly two years, and then suddenly she was back, as though nothing had happened. She wanted to be home, she said. I knew something had happened, we both did. She was in terrible shape. She didn't have a bag with her, just her purse. If we had known about you and your father . . . ' Jan trailed off, shaking her head and blinking away the tears.

'I know,' Lola said.

'And then she was gone,' Jan said. 'Dead.' The tears started in earnest. 'On the bad days, I still blame myself.'

Lola looked at Sam, whose face was shadowed in sympathy.

'You can't blame yourself that she was sick,' Lola said.

Jan nodded and held Lola's hands. 'We would have loved to have been part of your life, Lola. I hope you will include us a little now and then.'

'Of course,' said Lola, smiling.

'You've made this a little easier, losing Vivian. We're blessed to have you now,' Jan half-sobbed, hugging Lola close.

Lola hugged her back, understanding that they had lost a daughter and eighteen years of their only grandchild's life.

'Let's get some photos,' Sam said, fishing around for his digital camera.

Lola posed with Jan and Kevin, and then individually, and then Jan took photos of Lola and Sam, and Sam and Kevin. It felt endless to Lola, who was exhausted from the emotion of the past few weeks.

As the afternoon came to a close, Jan glanced at Kevin before clearing her voice. 'Darling, we want to give you something.'

'You don't have to give me anything,' Lola protested.

'We know, but Kevin and I discussed it as soon as we found out about you. First, I've put together a big box of your mother's things for you. Her diaries as a child, artwork, school reports. So you can get a glimpse of who she was.'

Lola nodded, a wave of emotion filling her heart.

'And, secondly, you are all we have, Lola. The only family left. So we've decided to give you the inheritance we would have left to your mother.'

'You don't need to do that,' Lola said quickly. Money was the last thing on her mind. She hated the idea that her newfound grandparents might think that was why she was there.

'We want to. We have enough money, and it's just sitting there. You could do something exciting with it,' said Jan. 'We would love to be able to help you. What's your dream? I'm sure you have a big dream.'

Lola looked at Sam, who smiled at her. 'You honestly don't need to give me money,' she said, turning to Jan.

'We've already decided. Please let us help you.'

Lola shook her head. 'I don't know what to say.'

'Say you'll be a part of our lives now,' said Jan anxiously.

'Money or no money, I will be a part of your lives,' Lola said. 'We're family.'

It felt good to say that, and Lola hoped it felt even better for her grandparents to hear.

Sam stood by the hire car, giving Lola some space as she placed a small bunch of pink roses on her mother's grave.

'So, hi,' Lola said to the gravestone, feeling awkward but also really wanting to say something. 'Yeah, so . . . I'm Lola, your daughter.' The breeze blew and Lola paused, trying to gather her scattered thoughts.

'I'm sorry you got sick, Mum,' she continued. And then the tears came. 'I'm sorry you didn't stay and I'm sorry I didn't get to know you. But I'm really glad you had me.'

She stopped, wiping her eyes and sniffling. She glanced over at Sam, who was leaning against the car.

'Anyway, if you meet a girl named Katherine up there, she's English, smart, with brown hair and pretty blue eyes? Tell her I'm looking after Sam. That's him over there. He looks after me too. It's nice. We're good together.' Lola sniffed again. 'Anyway, just be free and do your thing, whatever it is that you do wherever you are. Keep an eye on us, and make sure we're being good humans and stuff.'

Lola slowly turned from the grave and started to walk towards Sam.

'Look,' he called out to her, pointing up to the sky.

Lola looked up and saw two pink heart-shaped foil balloons, entwined by their strings and rising into the sky.

'They must have come off a grave,' Sam said.

'Perhaps,' Lola said, as she got into the car. But she preferred to think it was the sign she was waiting for from her mother – and maybe Katherine. Two pink hearts in the sky, watching over Lola and Sam.

28

Lola dreamt her mother burst out of a huge cupcake and yelled 'Lolapalooza' at her, streamers and glitter falling from the skies.

When she woke, Lola realised she wasn't crying. It was the first time that she could remember dreaming about her mum and not crying. All morning the dream stayed with her as she moved about the empty cafe.

'You okay?' asked Sam as they sipped the coffee that had been made in the kitchen, now that the coffee machine had been sold. She was staring out the back door.

'Yeah,' she turned to him. 'But it's so weird not being open. I don't know what Dad's going to do with the space.'

A couple of weeks earlier, David had decided he was done

with the cafe, and they had closed for the last time the day before.

Sam look around the kitchen a little sadly and then peered at her a little more closely. 'You sure you're okay?' he asked again.

'I'm just thinking about everything I have to do before I pick up Dad next week,' she said vaguely.

But as she took a taxi to the rehab centre later that day, she still couldn't shake the dream. As she walked down the now-familiar corridor to her dad's room, she thought about the feeling the dream had given her.

She opened her dad's door and peeped around the door into the room.

'Lola!' said her dad, excited to see her. 'Wait there.' He put up his hand to stop her at the doorway.

David grabbed his walking frame and pulled himself up into a standing position, his face wincing in pain. Lola made to step forward and help.

'Stay,' he commanded.

'I'm not a dog,' Lola snapped, but her bad humour shifted as David walked slowly towards her, using the frame, but not too much.

'Oh my god,' she said, her eyes filling with tears. 'That's incredible.'

'It's only walking,' said David, but he did look proud of himself. He turned and walked back to his seat and sat down gingerly.

'How are you, Lollipop?' he asked, as she pulled up a chair beside his.

'I'm okay,' she said slowly. Her father had always called her Lollipop, but what had her mother called her?

'What did Mum used to call me?'

David looked at her and frowned. 'Lola, Viola.' he said. 'Why?'

She shrugged, disappointment flooding her. 'I don't know, I was just wondering. So, I've been thinking . . . '

'Yes?'

'I've thought about this long and hard,' she said. 'It's just about all I've thought since I got back from Perth.'

Her dad's face was clouded with worry.

Lola swallowed and took a deep breath for courage and lifted her chin. 'I want to start my own business.'

David looked surprised, and then worried again. 'Darling, I'm just not in a position to —'

'I'm not asking for money, Dad,' she interrupted. 'I'd use the money Jan and Kevin gave me.'

Her dad sighed, thinking it through. 'Lola, you're only young. You have things to do, places to see. You don't want to be tied down like I was.'

Lola felt her mouth set in a tight line. 'I know I tied you down, but I'm not planning on having children.'

'You didn't tie me down, Lola,' her dad said firmly. 'You lifted me up.' He took her hands in his. 'It was the endless worry of the cafe, and trying to make ends meet that tied me down. Try and have a better life than that, Lola.'

'I don't want to run a cafe.'

'Then what?'

Lola took her hands away from his. 'I want to open a cupcake delivery service.'

'Huh?'

'I want to make the most delicious, girly, fancy cupcakes you've ever seen,' she said, warming to her pitch. 'And then I will send them out in my gorgeous cupcake van, which I am going to buy.'

'I thought you didn't want to be a chef?'

'I don't,' said Lola with a smile. 'I want to make cakes.'

David laughed and shook his head. 'Really?' he asked.

Lola reached down into her bag. 'Really,' she said as she took out a folder. 'Here is the business plan I've been writing. And here are my ideas for types of cakes I'd like to make, and delivery costs. And the rent on a commercial kitchen.'

David leafed through the papers while Lola sat, nervously awaiting his reaction.

Finally he put the papers down on his lap.

'Who'll drive the van?'

Lola reached down into her bag again and took out a plastic card and handed it to him. 'Me,' she said proudly.

'You got your licence? Well done, Lolly!'

'It's only my learner's, but it's a start.'

'David?' They both turned and saw a nurse in the doorway, a wheelchair in front of her. 'It's time for your physio.'

David pulled himself up on his frame before moving it to one side to clear the way to the wheelchair. Lola stood up and put her hand under one of his elbows.

Slowly her dad shuffled towards the wheelchair, turning to slump gingerly into it when he got closer.

'Wagons ho!' he said.

Lola leant down and kissed him. 'Will you think about my idea?'

David nodded. 'I will, Lollipop,' he said, waving back at her as the nurse wheeled him off down the hallway.

Lola stood watching her father's progress down the corridor. She had just turned to leave when she heard her dad call out. 'Lolapalooza!'

She turned, her heart beating fast.

'I just remembered,' he called. 'She called you Lolapalooza.'

As Lola walked out of the hospital, the tears streamed down her face. But when she saw herself in the window's reflection, she realised she had never looked happier.

29

Lola indicated and turned, driving carefully up the street. She pulled over in front of the cafe, where Sam, Jane, David, Babcia and Clyde stood waiting.

The van was pink, with a beautiful cupcake painted on the back door. *Lolapalooza* was written on the side in curly writing, and underneath in a neat print, *Spread the love, eat a cupcake.*

Lola jumped out of the van, opened the back door and made a sweeping movement with her arm.

'Allow me to present my new business, Lolapalooza Cupcakes.'

Her audience clapped and cheered.

'Oh my god,' she said, coming around to give everyone a kiss in turn. 'I can't believe how excited I am. I just got my first order for a school fete. They want five hundred assorted cupcakes.'

'We need champagne!' cried her dad.

Clyde went to get the champagne while Lola showed the others the inside of the van. It was decked out to carry hundreds of cupcakes at a time.

When Clyde returned with champagne, they all raised their glasses to Lola and took a sip.

'And to Lolapalooza Cupcakes,' Sam cried, and they raised their glasses again, this time at the little pink van.

They went inside the cafe and sat down on the milk crates that they had been using as chairs in the months since the cafe was cleared out.

Jane approached Lola with a box tied up with a hot pink ribbon. 'For you,' she said and pressed the box into Lola's hands.

'You shouldn't have!' she grinned at Jane. She undid the ribbon and lifted off the lid. She pulled back the pink tissue paper.

'I didn't,' laughed Jane. 'But my mother did.'

Lola held up a T-shirt with appliquéd cupcakes all over it.

'Oh my god, I love it,' cried Lola, and she ran into the kitchen to change. She came out wearing the T-shirt tied up at the waist.

'You don't have to wear it,' laughed Jane.

'I totally do,' said Lola. 'Take a photo and you can send it to her.'

Lola posed as Jane took the photo with her phone.

'It looks very nice,' said Babcia approvingly.

'If you're very lucky Mum might make you one,' said Jane as she winked at Lola. 'She's quite famous in Queensland for her T-shirts.' Lola caught Clyde nodding excitedly at Babcia.

The reconciliation between Baba and Clyde had been surprisingly easy. The emotion of learning of Vivian's death had let blame disappear and forgiveness rule.

Lola watched Sam as he moved about her loved ones. She knew something was up. He'd been tense, too quiet and distant, for days.

After talking to Jane and her father a little more about her plans for Lolapalooza, she took Sam outside to the small courtyard.

'What's going on?' she asked.

'What? Nothing,' said Sam, shaking his head a little too much for Lola's liking.

She narrowed her eyes at him. 'You're shaking your head like you have water in your ears.'

'I'm fine, honest.'

'Rubbish, as you would say. Tell me.'

'I don't want to talk about it now. Tomorrow, when this is over. I don't want to ruin your moment.'

'Sam,' Lola said. 'Tell me. Please.'

Sam looked ahead, his hands shoved into the pockets of his jeans. 'I have to go home for a while.'

That wasn't so bad. Lola moved to the milk crates and sat down. 'Okay. Why?'

'I need to see Mum, for a start. It's been nearly a year and she misses me. I miss her.'

A part of Lola started to worry. This was sounding like more than a little trip back home. 'Will you come back?'

'I will,' he said, coming to sit next to her and pulling her towards him.

Lola looked at the weeds growing between the cracks in the bricks. 'I don't want you to go,' she started to cry.

'Who's going where?' Lola looked up and saw her dad standing in the doorway.

'Sam's going back to London,' she said, pulling away from Sam and wiping her eyes.

David walked out, his champagne in one hand and his cane in the other. He looked quite steady.

'Forever?' he asked.

'No,' said Sam slowly. 'But I need to see my family. Sort out some things.'

'Well, make sure you come back,' said David. 'Because I know of a new restaurant that's opening in about three months. They're looking for an apprentice.'

Sam's eyes widened at this. 'Is it going to be any good?'

'The chef's the best I know,' said David, shrugging. 'Trained in Europe, worked in hatted places. He's older but still inspired.'

'Sounds amazing,' said Sam. 'Who's the chef?'

'Me.'

Lola gasped. 'Huh?'

'I'm opening up my own place,' said David. 'I've got the investors locked in. The builders booked. Early menus planned. We're going to turn the cafe into the best restaurant this city has ever known.'

'Oh my god,' said Lola excitedly. 'It's a total food bromance! I knew you two would be amazing together!'

Sam put out his hand. 'I'd love to accept the offer, sir,' he said in a formal voice.

'Please,' said David in a faux-bossy voice. 'Call me Chef.'

'Yes, Chef,' said Sam, grinning from ear to ear.

That night, when Lola was in bed, Sam lying next to her, she wrote a mental list of her goals.

- *Decorate flat*
- *Make YouTube video of cupcake van for Kevin & Jan*
- *Buy kitten*
- *Live life to fullest*

Life was amazing. And Lola knew she'd always feel sad that her mother had never experienced life this way; that she had missed out on so much.

Lola got out of bed and picked up the photograph of her mother that rested on her bedside table. She walked out into her dad's room and sat down on his neatly made bed. He had been staying at Jane's, where there were fewer stairs.

The photo in the frame was yellowing with age, and she reminded herself she should get it scanned before it deteriorated any more.

Kevin and Jan had given her many photos of Vivian, but this

was still the one that spoke to Lola the most. The one she had grown up looking at every day, wishing for her mum to come back, always wondering where she was and why she'd left.

Lola undid the back of the old frame, using a metal nail file to pry the clasps on the back up.

Underneath was folded piece of paper, with Lola's name on the front. Lola gasped in surprise.

Her hands shaking, Lola undid the paper and started to read.

Dearest Lolapalooza,

Do you know how much I love you? But it's as though I'm going mad. Some days I think I'll make it and then I have days when all I want to do is run and hide, make it all go away.

But when I look at you, everything seems less hazy.

If I do go away, I'll come back to you again. And if I can't, then I will send someone else to make sure you're okay.

You will be okay.

Sometimes, when I can prise you away from your grandmother, I sing to you and you sigh and nuzzle into me.

Do you know how much I love you?

I do.

Mummy

X

Lola wept as she reread the letter, and then folded it up carefully and put it back into the frame.

Her mother had kept her promise. She said if she couldn't

come back then she would send someone to make sure Lola was okay.

She wandered back into her bedroom and looked at Sam, sleeping soundly, his mouth slightly open and his eyelashes fluttering. She leant down and kissed his cheek.

'Thank you,' she whispered to Sam and then looked at the photo, now back in its place next to her bed. 'And you were right. I am okay.'

30

It wasn't until she knew the truth about her mother that Lola could finally let her go.

Over time she stopped scanning crowds for red-headed women who might be her mother.

She stopped searching for her mother on the internet, and she no longer scrolled through London theatre reviews for an actress called Vivian.

And it wasn't until she stopped that she realised how much of her life she had put into the search.

Now Lola woke early, her feet hitting her bedroom floor with excitement at what lay ahead. She had so many ideas for cupcakes, and the orders were already rolling in for events big and small.

She was soon written up in the newspaper as the coolest girl in town, the 'Sweetheart of Cakes'. Lola said she didn't have time to read the article, but Babcia and Clyde had framed it for her and hung it in the flat.

When Lola drove around in her van she was proud of the interested looks she received, and she loved the happy waves. Her cupcake van felt like happiness on wheels.

It was nearly perfect. Nearly, because Sam was still away. It had been four weeks, and Lola missed him more than she could have ever imagined.

But he wasn't gone forever, as he kept reminding her when they Skyped. She'd even Skype-met his family.

He sent her pictures of cakes in the shops on the high streets and told her about cake businesses in London.

But none of this made it easier for Lola.

Sam had promised to be back for the opening of the restaurant. But Lola had a gnawing feeling, no matter what sensible advice she gave herself, that Sam wouldn't return. That the texts would gradually come less and less, the Skyping would drop away, that life in London would eventually win out for Sam.

The cafe refurbishment was in full swing. It was lucky Lola was too busy to be in the flat upstairs much, because downstairs was a noisy hive of activity. Builders and plumbers were to-ing and fro-ing every day, and Clyde was working to find the right blend of antiques to go with the modern fittings.

Lola threw herself into work to stop fretting about Sam.

She took on every order that came her way, and was now looking to hire some part-time help in the kitchen.

What she missed most about Sam was their friendship. They'd been friends first, and losing that was harder than Lola had expected.

'Maybe we were just meant to be together right then, to push each other forward in life. You know, friends for a reason or a season or whatever that saying is,' she had said to Sarah and Rosie during a girls' night at the flat.

Rosie played with Minty, the new kitten. 'I don't think so.'

'That's because you're a romantic,' Lola had scoffed.

'No, I just think what you and Sam have is bigger than that,' said Rosie, calmly prising Minty's little claws from her jumper.

'How's your dad?' asked Sarah as she refilled their wine glasses and helped herself to another of Lola's mini-cupcakes.

'He's good, seems to be loving living with Jane. They're full on into the restaurant, trying to open on time.'

'What's it called again?' asked Rosie.

'Vivian's,' Lola said, smiling. 'After my mum. Dad said she always wanted to see her name in lights, and now it will happen.'

'God, I'm going to cry,' said Rosie as she lifted Minty off her lap to let her play.

'Was Jane okay with that?' asked Sarah.

'She was fine, believe it or not. Jane's amazing, the best thing that ever happened to Dad. Even Babcia likes her. She's knitting her a jumper with cows on it,' said Lola with a laugh. She was truly happy for them. They were a joy to be around, so caring and kind to each other.

But after Sarah and Rosie had left, and Lola sat in her flat with only Minty and the leftover cupcakes for company, she wondered why she was always the one left all alone.

31

It was the morning of the restaurant opening, and Lola woke up feeling calm.

Something within her had shifted, she noticed. Her first thought wasn't about Sam, and she didn't check her phone for messages from him.

Instead she showered and dressed in a cute skirt with flamingos on it, and a pink crop top. She slipped on her white canvas sneakers, and had just begun to walk downstairs when she heard a noise from the kitchen.

No-one should be here yet, she thought, freezing on the stairs and listening. Were they being broken into?

She was about to creep upstairs for her old hockey stick from school, to use as a weapon, when she heard the sound of the industrial mix master.

What sort of a thief whips up a batch of cupcakes at seven in the morning? She peered around the corner and screamed.

'Sam!' She leapt down the last few stairs and ran towards him.

He caught her in his arms and kissed her. He tasted like chocolate.

'What are you doing here?' Lola demanded, in between kisses. 'I thought you arrived this afternoon!'

'I got on an earlier flight. I want to help out. I'm so nervous I haven't been able to think of anything else.'

Lola laughed as she kissed his face all over. 'You're funny.'

'And you're lovely,' he answered as she felt him pull her towards the bench. 'I love you, Lola,' he asked huskily into her ear.

She pulled back to look at him. 'Sam, I have to ask. Why did you leave? I mean, really?' It was something she'd spent many hours wondering since he'd left.

Sam took her face in his hands. 'I had to see Katherine's grave, one more time. And I had to see her family again. I guess I wanted them to know that I was moving on, but that didn't mean I'd forgotten Katherine. Or that I ever would.' He looked at Lola nervously, obviously worried about how she'd react to this.

Lola flung her arms around him again, pulling him tight.

Later, when they lay in Lola's bed, Sam held her hand up to his mouth and kissed each of her fingers in turn.

'I told my Mum that I was in love with you,' he said.

'Oh?' Lola smiled and then made a face. 'And?'

'She said she thought as much when she met me at the airport,' said Sam. 'She wondered if it was the Australian sun, but I explained it was the Australian girls.'

'Girls?' Lola tried to pull her hands away.

'Girl,' he said firmly. 'One girl. Lola, from Melbourne.'

Lola kissed him and her stomach flipped with desire all over again.

'You know I'm totally falling for you, don't you?' she whispered in his ear.

'Oh I fell a long time ago,' he said as he moved down her body, kissing each freckle that he found along the way.

'When?' she asked, as he kissed her stomach.

'When you held my hand by the river, that's when I was sure,' he said, looking up at her.

'You're such a romantic,' she said as he moved down, planting slow kisses along the way.

'Do you ever stop talking?'

'Not unless someone can shut me up,' said Lola, her laugh turning into a soft gasp as his head moved between her legs, and his tongue flickered down further.

'Okay,' she said as Sam worked his way down the inside of her thigh and then back up again. 'That might shut me up.' She grasped the sheets as the pleasure became almost too much. She finally had Sam exactly where she wanted him.

32

TWELVE MONTHS LATER

'Do you take this woman, to have and to hold, for richer, for poorer, in sickness and in health, to love and to cherish, from this day forward until death do you part?'

'I do.'

'Do you take this man, to have and to hold, for richer, for poorer, in sickness and in health, to love and to cherish, from this day forward until death do you part?'

'I do.'

'You may now kiss one another.'

Lola shifted a little, the baby growing heavy in her arms.

A huge cheer came from the crowd and Lola felt her eyes fill with tears as she kissed the downy head of the baby. She felt her father's arms around her and the baby.

'Congratulations,' she said to her dad, crying and laughing at the same time. She moved to Jane, who hugged her tightly as baby Max started to cry a little.

'What are you crying about?' Jane asked she took her son from Lola's arms.

'He misses his mum,' said Lola, touching Max's chubby cheek.

'He needs to get used to lots of people loving him,' said Jane as she made funny faces at the baby.

'But there's no-one like mumma,' said Lola, and at that Jane put her free arm around her again.

'I know I'm not your real mum, but I love you like you're my own,' said Jane.

Lola's eyes welled up with happiness. Jane had become a confidante, a friend and, at times, yes, even a mother to Lola. Lola cherished every moment of their new connection. When Max was born it just cemented the bond. Lola was at the birth, which had been amazing – although, after seeing how hard childbirth was, she told Sam she would be adopting any children in her future.

'I never thought I could be this happy, Lola,' Jane whispered in her ear.

Lola swallowed her tears, the emotion almost overwhelming her.

'I love you and I love how you love Dad,' she managed to get out before someone pushed her aside and Lola found herself on the outside of the circle of well-wishers.

She glanced at the table lined with champagne glasses and, resplendent in the middle, the wedding cake. Lola had made it herself, and it had taken days. A bottom layer of lemon cake, then a layer of her best chocolate mud, and then the top layer of angel food cake.

It was all covered in kisses of vanilla butter cream icing with tiny yellow sugar daisies scattered across it. On top were little figurines of Jane and David, also made from icing, including David's walking stick that he still used when his hips were hurting.

Lola watched as Sanjay pushed her grandfather, Kevin, around in his wheelchair, chatting to him. She saw Jan gossiping with Jane's mother. Clyde and Babcia were talking to the happy couple, and Rosie was posing for Sarah's camera as the sound of the DJ started up.

Dancing and cake were what Jane had requested for the reception, and so they were married in the courtyard of the restaurant, with the dancing to commence inside.

Lola moved into the kitchen to make sure the staff were filling the champagne glasses. Standing beside the DJ in the empty cafe, Lola took a moment, knowing that soon the party would surge inside and start to dance, filling the space with laughter and stupid dance moves. She felt good in her sequined mint-coloured dress. It was short and cute and just right. She did a twirl to the music, enjoying the feeling as the bass filled her ears and started to pulse through her. She threw her head back and laughed, and decided suddenly to clamber up onto the communal table.

There's something to be said about living in the moment and remembering that the best time is the one you're having right now, she thought as she closed her eyes and moved to the track that was playing. Lost in the music, Lola put her arms up and then she felt arms around her, pulling her tight.

'Hello,' she said, as she opened her eyes.

Sam kissed her neck.

'Where have you been?'

'Prepping first course,' he said, slurring his words a little. 'You taste like lemon icing.'

'You're a cheap shout,' she laughed. 'You're already half-pissed.'

The room started to fill with others as Sam danced with her on the table until she felt him nearly fall off and take her with him.

'Get off the table,' she ordered him. Sam jumped down in one fluid movement, and put his arms up in the air for her, to a roar of approval from Sarah and Rosie, who were dancing nearby.

Lola jumped into his arms as gracefully as she could. He swung her around and into a low dip, nearly tipping them both onto the floor.

'I used to think I was the crazy one,' she laughed as she and Sam spun around to the song.

'I'm crazy. You're crazy, everyone's crazy.' He looked at her closely, his green eyes wide. 'And I'm crazy about you, Viola Batko.'

'And I'm crazy about you Sam Button.'

'You know, if we got married, you'd be Lola Button.'

'Hang on, Mister Button, no proposal yet, okay? I'm a career woman, I've got a business to run. And anyway, who says I'd change my name?'

'Fair point,' Sam laughed and spun her around, and then pulled her close. 'You know how proud of you your mum would be, don't you?'

Lola looked at everything around her. David and Jane, slow dancing despite the heavy beat, Clyde and Babcia sipping their champagne and bobbing out of time, Kevin and Jan looking delighted to be there.

'I know, but you know what?'

'What?' asked Sam as he played with one of her curls.

She smiled and wrapped her arms around his neck. 'Most of all, I'm proud of myself. And that feels better than anything else in the world.'

Sam's hands slid around her waist, pulling her to him, and she could feel how much he wanted her.

'Anything?' he asked, desire in his eyes.

'Almost anything,' she said cheekily, and then they kissed, surrounded by everyone who loved them.

Check out the rest of the Smitten series – available as books and ebooks now!